Ib's Endless Search for Satisfaction

ROSHAN ALI

PENGUIN

VIKING

An imprint of Penguin Random House

VIKING

USA | Canada | UK | Ireland | Australia
New Zealand | India | South Africa | China

Viking is part of the Penguin Random House group of companies
whose addresses can be found at global.penguinrandomhouse.com

Published by Penguin Random House India Pvt. Ltd
7th Floor, Infinity Tower C, DLF Cyber City,
Gurgaon 122 002, Haryana, India

Penguin
Random House
India

First published in Viking by Penguin Random House India 2019

ISBN 9780670092383

Typeset in Garamond by Manipal Digital Systems, Manipal
Printed at Replika Press Pvt. Ltd, India

www.penguin.co.in

Ib's Endless
Search for Satisfaction

ADVANCE PRAISE FOR THE BOOK

'Roshan Ali's prose is an exhilarating dream ride through a city of memory and desire, mixing Emily Dickinson with *tapori* English, while remaining true to a central truth: we only know what we know when we know how we know it'—Jerry Pinto, author of *Em and the Big Hoom* and *Murder in Mahim*

To my parents, who let me be,
And to Arpi, who didn't.

PART 1

Perhaps, perhaps, perhaps.
—song

ONE

I am an empty man in an empty city, and every time I begin to fill up, the city sucks it all out again. An empty city is the subject—the subject of everything—and I am the object. What is it about cities that empties me like this? Maybe it's the density, the fullness, stuffed with people of such lofty stuffing that the natural technique of nature to empty the filled and to fill the empty is reversed by this overdose of man and his mischief; and thus a thin man like me gets the stuffing sucked out of him, till he is hollow and restless. So it is necessary for any objects that move about a city to have these lofty notions of man and society, to contribute, to fit in and thus avoid the mad dissatisfaction of being hollow. A samosa, as someone once said, is better stuffed than empty, whatever the stuffing, if only to give you some satisfaction that you're getting what you're paying for, leave the side effects aside.

Some things are certain. Like, death is certain. I know death because it is certain and all around, though sneaky, invisible, oddly so for something this black and big and this is another thing about cities: how they hide death. But I have never experienced death, never seen death. Yet I know death is painful. Death is dark and deep and does not stop because it has so much to do. Death—that thing with feathers—comes out from the unknown, leaps on to the road, sticks and stones ready, and leaves you bloody and a broken nose. It is only afterwards that you know: Death was there all along, crouching by the side of the road, and became known only when it jumped out into your headlights.

History is certain too—maybe it is a lie, told by the ones who know how to lie, or a nightmare—but it is certain. These things that are certain—death, history—don't really need to be told because they are well known. My history is well known to me—the only one who needs to know—and I go about things (but wait, that's been told), but must be repeated. I am like lighter fluid—easily flammable—yet I require that spark, the right temperature and conditions. And in many ways isn't that better? Where would you store such a lighter fluid that combusts itself in regular weather and pleasant rooms? Thus I begin: I am Indian, city-born—cities, those empty cities—and go about things . . . but that's enough. And not really true.

Where should I begin? The signs of my birth were absent. I came, plonk! and the nurse was surprised. It is possible that her mind was briefly distracted into attention by this entity shaped like a peanut. At once she must have thought about weakness. Something so magical for the parents; so dull to her that her mind was almost at once back to some boy or the other, and nail polish, or the evening. Also, nobody cares about things that have no signs (except signs themselves which seldom have signs, and if they do, to propose that these signs had signs too would be stretching any reasonable rights to speculate. A sign of a sign is utter confusion: Imagine a road with an infinite regression of signs. Where will they end? Or rather, where will they begin? These are questions worth asking.). And speaking of this, there must be some connection with our lives, some hints, some clues of uniqueness, or blessing. Maybe, in the old, black, round-bum Fiat, many weeks before my slimy, unmiraculous birth, Amma said, tapping Appoos's shoulder and pointing towards the sky, 'Look, Kamran, that cloud looks like a boy!' And father replied: 'All the clouds or just that one?' And mother said, 'Shtap, no. You always make fun of me. But see, it can be a sign.' These things are fun: The stars wait quietly in their silent formation; nothingness heaves a deep sigh; and time is released like a river of red confetti into the darkness of space, like a trumpet of victory for every unique, human peanut occasion; and thus forming the universe itself. And like this every day, universe after universe is born and then dies. These are the stuffings of excitement, and I've been told—there are many who make it their business to do so—that I rip the stuffings out of excitement wherever I go. This is my fate: To not only be a blanket soaked in some universal ether of grimness, but to rip the stuffing out of whatever kind of exciting mattress is being used in that particular venue. I have been called many things—fun

5

isn't one of them. In fact, here is another lie—I have never been called anything but my one name. Perhaps, this is a sign of a miserable life: I am the one-headed, one-brained, monkey-eared, one-named, one. And in the event that you are still hoping for magic and mystery: No there were no signs of my birth, and allied to tedium and every expectation, I wasn't born any time even close to midnight.

My mother had a nice face, a nice ear; the other ear not so nice and quite normal. She was nice—a deceptively small word that is exactly as simple as it sounds—and never yelled at any servant, and even refused to call them that. Sometimes she had two baths a day. Father, father deluded, was mad as a flag in a storm, was rocking crazy and fun in his own crazy way. He went nuts shortly after my birth, and nobody seemed to know why. But is there a why to these things? And I sometimes wonder if I am going to go mad too sometime in the dim future (the future is always dim). Thus I had no father, or no fatherly father, thus no father, and fatherless I found my own patrons. There was Nooby, the wise, old, sexually excited ant; Frauntfraunty, a cancer-stricken housemouseelf ('Metastasized master, metastasized,' he used to say); BringOverMarty, the once popular sitcom star from one of those United States who now managed a dhobi ghat and spoke in riddles ('I wring-a-wring-a rose dress, bring-a-bring-a coal-grey dress. Is this yours? Is this yours? Is this yours?') which weren't really riddles but possessed a manner of rhythm and tune; and finally, Shaktidas Murali Broom, a retired *besom* with an unusually straight back who understood the deep, complex problems of life but alas, could never articulate himself ('God make naise too much, he not ther. Man make noise too much, he ther, but aalvays he try disafeer. Naat nice.').

Amma, with her nice, oval face and tiny height, survived. Sometimes, and even Darwin said, survival is a matter of fitness, yet mother was never fit—though her hair was remarkably black and neat. She was Hindu by birth (or so she was told), nothing by choice, then Buddhist by choice and songbird by next birth—this is what she believed. Amma, shortly after father went mad, went quietly sane, saner than she had ever been, and forgot her dreams of being reborn as a songbird. She was a quiet, sane woman after that, never looking at clouds. Sometimes I recall her nice face, through the steamed lens of childhood by my bedside, as Shaktidas Murali Broom sat, straight-backed, listening (he never interrupted—this is a sign of a good friend). She spoke for hours softly. I don't remember much—the past is dim—yet I remember her hands contained in her lap and her mouth moving slowly; her sad, neat mouth and her very white, clean teeth. One evening as she left my room, Shaktidas said in my ear, 'Human bean many sadness. Heavy, heavy harat.' And Nooby, who was hiding in the closet, stuck his head out and added, 'Dude, you have a very beautiful mother; if I had little more strength . . . and in this old age . . . difficult to move. But I would really give it to her right in the . . .' And BringOverMarty appearing suddenly beside my thin legs cut him short. 'Quiet ant, stupid ant, lingers over things. Quiet boy, bright boy, what's your heart think?'

he sang. And I said to myself, 'One day I will make my mother a machine that will listen to her stories and give her high fives.' Nobody laughed and everything was quiet. Quietness occupied a large part of my childhood.

Amma was, above all things, one who avoided conflict and everything, like herself and her room, was clean and she believed in not talking about things. Conflict—that pins-and-needles feeling that comes with every position a man takes for too long—was quite efficiently swept under rugs and other warm things like caramel pudding. And everyone knows spiky things must never be swept under rugs: Often, when it was least expected, these things pierced through and slowly tearing apart, exploded into the quiet living room space. Appoos was mad after all, and one couldn't sustain a fight too long, as it collapsed over the weakness of one party to maintain a point over the course of even one sentence; so the shouting faded only to be replaced with a strained and tight peace in the air, a volatile mixture that was set-off at the least signs of trouble. It followed that there was not much talking in our home lest this strange peace was disturbed and I spent my days in this or that world. Amma also often did things to make herself feel better regardless of the final product, which was counter-productive because it was the final product, usually, that affected her.

Her husband, Appoos—called Kamran by everyone other than his son; once a stout and upright guy with an impressively maintained moustache and hard, thick arms, but now a shrivelled and fluttery fellow who rarely stood up—was harmlessly schizophrenic, and was good company when there was nothing serious to discuss. But when critical topics were brought up, there was only that laugh; that merciless, non-discriminatory laugh; and this tore up Amma, who was trying to take life seriously. There was no place for humour in Amma's life: Her wounds were too grave for laughter to be any kind of medicine. In those days, when she was patient, and when Appoos and her ate together (later he ate alone, and watched something through the window), she would quietly tell him to pay attention, to quiet down, to be normal, as if his madness was just another state of his annoying mind that could be reasoned with, to be told off and controlled by words. He was terrified—of what we didn't know—and I felt scared too. The table at meals was always cold with an unspoken tension. Sometimes, when Appoos had an episode, it was like our quotidian family dinner was interrupted by a rakshasa in work clothing, all ready to kill, but disguised as an office man (and if you looked carefully, the blood glinted red in the white of the light under his perfect length blazer-sleeve), and mother's jaw would clench and something inside her would begin to swell and make her hands shake. Then, like she normally did, when things began to explode, she would leave. I wondered if everything would be better if my mother did just hit him. That poor woman—maybe she needed the violence, the licence for violence. Maybe violence can save lives. And is there anything worse than people happy for no reason? I mostly hated mental Appoos but pretended not to—that's the truth; I swear on my father.

Appoos had good days and bad, but this was what he said and we all knew most days were bad though this wasn't really his fault and came down usually to the net amount of seriousness in the universe. I, little coward, was never around; usually in my room trying to get rid of seriousness, and bad things, by swatting at them like one would do against flies and other motley creatures with wings; distractedly dodging and swiping at these bad things that I somehow sensed in the world but could never explain, or articulate.

I don't really remember much of a small, conveniently close school, perhaps because my mind had driven out the stuff that made it untidy, a nervous mess, but I remember a cane and a sharp pain, but nothing more and nobody's face to put it to. Often it is just a kind of sharp, painful fog, somewhere in the space of my mind, the rest of which tries its best to forget those smoggy days.

I was told much later that one day, there was a mark on my arm. Amma saw it while changing my shirt and she screamed and cried and I screamed and cried and the next morning there was no school, and I was overjoyed, running up and down the stairs.

What I remember is, I came back every evening from that school, before mother made a fuss and took me out, and there was a tune. It went like this. *Na, Na, Na, Na, Na, Na, Na.* Shaktidas liked it, even though he said he didn't, but I knew it moved him, like it moved me. It moved something deep inside me, physically and solidly. I felt something shift inside, in the unknowable spaces between thoughts and ideas, feelings and actions. The tune came from a piano in a corner, from lonely hands somewhere in the neighbourhood. But then one day it was gone (I have found that things usually do). And then I relied on Shaktidas; I would say to him, 'Hey, Broom (this annoyed him). Sing that song, na.' And he would sing, *na na na na na na*, but it was over much too fast, much too swiftly. These are the things that really annoy me: the good things that get over too soon and perhaps the bad ones that linger.

The oddly scented, dimly lit mist of the past has obscured much, and I can barely remember some things, and yet others remain clear, perhaps a little too clear. Like that house we lived in: Completely white on the outside, and completely dull, with a flat roof, flat walls, flat everything. The door, which I can feel even now, was rough and heavy and made of some reddish wood and smelt of polish. Bars criss-crossed every entrance, every potential entrance; black, hard, shining, and obscured every opening into the world with a jail-like texture. Inside. The furniture was dull, faded cloth on unpolished wood, and smelt of old things left alone for too long. A long, narrow corridor led from the door to the dim insides of this animal that I was raised in. A kitchen clanked further on, and to the left a neglected guest bedroom, unused for years. To the right, a narrow staircase that took you past cobwebs. Upstairs. A large bedroom with the lightness of my mother's scent, arranged and neat, and attached, through a corridor, past the bathroom that nobody used, a tiny room, mine, with

11

a view of empty plots, and far away, a road, and far away, buildings, and far away, the city.

I also recollect an uncle with nothing, who visited once a year; an uncle from some cold, snowy country with signs of air travel hanging off huge suitcases. He brought shiny shoes, shell-shaped chocolates, till he lost his money—as it inevitably leaves—and then brought keychains and empty boxes and gave them to me with the same eagerness, with the same words and the same expression, as if, if he pretended, nobody would notice how poor he had become. Foreign Uncle—this wasn't his name—smoked like a dragon and I am aware that dragons are extinct. Of course this is beside the point. He was outspoken in a careless way, and around him people found themselves fidgeting very often. While Amma was like this and grimaced and shuffled when Foreign Uncle brought up sex—which he very often did because he said I needed to be 'well versed and knowing' on these things—Appoos laughed, and he was probably a liberal in the way that he wasn't against anything really. Some forbidden topics often started a strange argument between them: Appoos couldn't really argue, but Amma having an easy opponent, continued to force points. And while this one-sided debate occurred, Foreign Uncle, smoking a cigarette, and resting his hairy arm on the chair I sat on, smiled and coughed.

One day, it was Saturday evening, late March, cornering me in the corridor next to the bathroom that nobody used, he reached into his shirt and brought out a long box of Marlboro cigarettes. I had seen the long boxes before, in the glass windows of shopping malls, a red and white brick, so crisp and foreign, and of course, by that point, I was 'well versed and knowing' on this topic of nicotine, but the look on my face betrayed my nervousness, because never before had nicotine and my mother been in such close proximity (she was maybe ten feet away below me, putting out dinner). He handed them over quietly, his eyes darting towards the door behind me. 'You better hide them,' he said quietly. 'And not before you're fifteen.' Then he walked past quickly and I heard his heavy steps going down the stairs and then his muffled voice as he innocently asked Amma a question about dinner.

I didn't understand then why Foreign Uncle had given me that box of cigarettes. I was only twelve, and had only just begun to discover the twin pleasures of nicotine and rebellion. And of course I assumed all the adults were part of some worldwide undercover operation to crack down on teenage smoking. But apparently Foreign Uncle wasn't one of these strict, rule-loving adults, and I immediately liked him more for it. And now it was our little secret to glance at about over dinner or tea. And of course I never told him that I smoked almost immediately after he gave me the cigarettes, on the terrace, braving the sun. But say what you want about Foreign Uncle, he wasn't a stupid man. He certainly knew I would smoke, and gave them to me despite this. Years later, when I told Major, he said, 'He obviously wanted you to smoke, Ib. He wanted to set you free from your parents.' This made sense. After all, he was miserable like all the adults, and maybe he was trying

13

to live through me, his only young relative, and gain some joy by setting me free.

Foreign Uncle was Amma's brother. He was younger by a few indistinguishable years. Amma never liked him much. He's always complaining, she said. And he was— constantly irritated and grumpy about matters that he couldn't control, depressed about some state of affairs in a country I didn't know existed, but unwilling to think beyond his anger and frustration.

In the winter of some year, the last night of his annual trip to the country of his birth and the last time I saw him, he came home late and drunk and smelling of smoke. Amma was upset when she opened the door and went upstairs without saying a word. She was too upset to even put me to bed, so I sat there on the landing and watched his clayey frame standing still in the living room, till he heard Amma's door shut, then he sat heavily on the sofa and closed his eyes. Then he rose and walked around, stopping occasionally at a picture on the wall, or at the fish tank with its three still-alive fish, and artificial plants. All at once, as the orange light from a street lamp outside fell on his shapeless face, I seemed to see beneath his expression and his form, and suddenly felt a deep sadness that I had never felt before. And suddenly I felt angry at mother for being so upset and insensitive. Couldn't she see how miserable he was? He was so lonely and sad. He seemed to sense my presence, and called out softly. I went down the stairs on my toes. He sat down and lit a cigarette. 'Did you see?' he asked, not looking at me. I nodded and he sighed. 'Forget it, Ib. You shouldn't worry about such things. At least not yet.' He smiled. 'Don't you have school tomorrow? Go, go. To bed.' I scampered up the stairs, and before I reached the landing, I turned and glanced one last time at my sad uncle. He hadn't moved, still sitting there, looking down at the floor.

Later at night as I lay in bed, Shaktidas Broom, who had been attending to personal problems all day, came and sat beside me. 'Man,' he said, 'is monkey. But he naat know. That is problem.'

The next morning, my uncle was gone and I never saw him again.

* * *

Every time Foreign Uncle left, there was suddenly another kind of quiet. He was a bit crazy too, sometimes. Stories floated around among relatives who had nothing else to do: Once he invited people for a party, then locked himself in the toilet till the guests left, perplexed. Another time, he made a stack of photographs and took photographs of the stack and made a stack of those. The word was that he was crazy anyway. But the relative who sometimes dropped in for tea usually made it a point to distinguish Appoos's real madness to this pretend nuttiness that Foreign Uncle displayed. 'He's lonely, no,' they said. 'He can become depressed'; as if loneliness leads to sadness. 'There is a tendency for solitary people to become depressed,' said one distant, pale uncle with strange wrists who was a local doctor, but I didn't pay much attention because only his friends went to him.

15

Tea was served with a sense of occasion, but mild occasion because one must always be careful about the level of occasion and because on all occasions there is someone disappointed. Amma knew about disappointment. Tea was generally served with snacks; and was tea and snacks but just called tea. This was another domestic euphemism commonly applied and there were many others that I cannot recollect. Sometimes Amma, depending on her mood and independent of our appetites, made entire meals or just a few biscuits. Appoos ate without trouble, belching and enunciating every detail of his process. I found it difficult sometimes, but with Amma there was no way of avoiding. She never asked and was always serving and taking for granted that I would eat everything that was served. 'You're getting thin. Eat. Clean your plate. Or you'll get pointy like barbed wire,' she always said. And Appoos laughed a bloated laugh with things coming out of his mouth. As luck would have it, and maybe the universe had something to do with it, I never grew fat and never have, despite my natural laziness. Later, somebody said to me, 'You think too much. All your food is going away to feed your imaginary persons.' Such is my physical form.

* * *

As a quiet child, I had many dreams. I dreamt I would become a star-traveller, hopping galaxies, fixing dying suns, watering dry planets, freeing a people. I dreamt I would be an electric god, lighting currents in all the dark parts of the world, giving light to darkness, freshness to mouldy areas, with just a wave of my hand. And finally that I would become a singer of magical songs, with words that mended bloody wounds and a tune that calmed the worst of wars.

Shaktidas was always supportive of all my dreams and even gave me suggestions on how to achieve them. 'You start drawing,' he used to say. 'Drawings are path to greatness.' And so I drew: I drew the stars and the planets, galaxies and black holes, even the universe, and me in a black astronaut suit, floating about, not to scale.

When Amma found these drawings she was struck by how dull they were, but it amused her and she used to smile and go through them one by one. 'Aren't there more colours in the universe, babu?' she asked me once. 'Not visible to the human eye,' I replied.

She said, 'So what? Why don't you just colour them? They'll look so pretty.'

'I don't want to draw lies. I want to draw the truth.'

'OK, babu,' she said, amused, exasperated, and tender at the same time. 'You draw the truth, but what's the point if the truth is dull? Isn't there enough of that all around us?' And as she finished the sentence her face fell, and she got up, letting the drawing slip from her hand on to the floor. She was back in her Appoos mode, the mode in which she took care of things. There was no joy in that mode. 'Do the dishes later, OK? Ratna is not coming tomorrow,' she said and went out, closing the door behind her, as if to preserve the relative happiness that was present inside my room. Shaktidas crawled out from under the bed and stretched out his back. 'Need draw colours, Ib,' he said, 'or else you are sadden your mummy.'

17

'It's not my problem that she's so miserable.'

'She is mummy or not? Mummy are always son's problem.'

'If only I had a sister. She would take care of Amma and I could go on drawing things. And where am I going to get colours from?' I cried.

'There's a shop by the bridge,' Nooby said.

'Nooby, where have you been? Do you think I should add more colours?

'Look, Ib,' said Nooby seating himself comfortably on the floor. 'You know what I feel about your mother. I think she needs a good . . .'

'Hey, yenough,' Shaktidas said angrily. He glared at Nooby, who couldn't have cared less.

'Fine,' he said shrugging his shoulders, 'you asked for my opinion. No banging? Then, certainly, add some colour to her life. This is the only colour she has.'

And then suddenly, Nooby disappeared. Right in front of my eyes; one second there he was, and the next, he was gone. I jumped out of bed and rummaged through the cupboard but he wasn't there. 'Shaktidas, where the hell did Nooby go?' I asked and turned to look at Broom, but he was nowhere to be found either. The others too were gone and the room felt empty. Fearful of my life, I hid under the blankets and fell asleep. Later, when I woke up, it was the middle of the night and to my relief, Shaktidas was asleep on his favourite shelf.

I took their advice to heart (perhaps because of their strange disappearing act), and the next morning I told my mother my immediate desire for colours. She pressed some notes into my small palm.

'Take a left by the bridge, it's next to the chicken shop,' she said, 'and talk with respect to Sharmaji. He knows your father.'

I remember there was an unusual cold in the air that morning. But it wasn't that unusual because it was the beginning of winter, and a cold was beginning to form in the sky. In the empty plot on my street a line of silver oaks stood up tall and straight, grey swaying sentries, shushing sternly at the breeze, made to watch over abandoned land. Below them a pig had made a nest and was leading a line of piglets across the road towards their home. Eager and afraid, they bumped into the back of their siblings, all rushing to catch up with their muddy mother. Further on, by the bridge, a mad man roamed the street, shouting at strangers. When he saw me he smiled and I hurried past.

Here's Sharmaji, an oiled, shapeless man, with dents in his fleshy arms like the ones on an overripe papaya. He wore a dull gold shirt, a bright gold chain and an even brighter gold watch, and watched a cricket match on a tiny television on a shelf, muttering occasionally to himself and complaining to his assistant—'The state of Indian cricket I tell you, these days. Arre, Mahesh, look at this guy, yaar, he's so bad. Why is he in the team?' And Mahesh's job was to agree—'He doesn't know anything. Kick him out.'

'Somebody is paid, some match-fixing.'

'Everything is fixed, sir.'

They shook their head in exasperated wisdom.

I called out and they turned and for a second they couldn't see me. Then Sharmaji spotted my head over the counter and said impatiently, pushing something red to one side of his mouth, 'What do you want?' and without waiting for my reply, went back to watching the match, clucking with wise disappointment.

Unfazed, I set out my list on the counter and waited. He picked it up, his eyes still glued to the screen.

'Poster coloursh? Watercoloursh?' he asked, his 's's smooshed into 'sh's by that devil shit in his mouth (Appoos's term).

'Uncle, what can I use on paper?'

He sighed and spat out a red blob that flew past my head on to the pavement. 'Beta, you can use anything you want,' he said, his turgid face finally turned towards me. 'You want a light finish, use watercolours, you want solid finish, use the poster colours. But I suggest poster colours because they are easier. My children always use poster colours. My daughter is your age only. How old are you? Yes, correct. My son, he's older. But very good at studies. Where do you stay? Kamran's son? What's your name? Ib, what name is that? Muslim name must be. Me and Kamran, same college. What happened to him, yaar? I must come and visit.'

Mahesh, the assistant, had meanwhile collected the colours and placed them on the counter. 'Choose,' he said grumpily.

I did, pointing them out one by one with my finger. At the level of my eye, the colours were bright and solid like small skyscrapers. Red, blue, green, orange, yellow.

The assistant wrapped them in newspaper and put them in a bag.

'Thank you, uncle,' I said after paying, but he paid no attention and Mahesh grumbled and waved me away. On my way home, the mad man was sitting on the roadside talking to himself. 'Shruti said that, yes, Shruti said to go away. Where is Shruti, where is she?' he was saying, over and over again. I hurried past and once beyond those tall silver oaks, I felt safe.

* * *

It seemed to my small and innocent brain that Nooby, Shaktidas and the others were going for sudden and short vacations. They would suddenly disappear in the middle of conversations, games, debates. I felt that maybe they were going to do some grown-up things, involving girls, beer and cigarettes, so I never brought it up. And they never spoke about it either because, I assumed, they didn't want to make me feel bad about the whole thing. I was still a child after all.

I was around ten when Nooby disappeared one day and never came back. It was one of those days, the kind of day that feels strange in retrospect, because our minds are made in such a way as to see connections where none exist and to see coincidence in randomness, meaning in meaninglessness. Such as it was, I had no feeling of strangeness on that day, but now after all these years, coloured by the sepia lenses of nostalgia, that melancholy of oldness, a yearning for lost things, all combined in fateful ways to produce the kind of feeling that makes you think the past matters more than it actually does. Such is the way that life revolves.

It was a Tuesday, I think, but accuracy of memory has been replaced by feelings, and it might have been Wednesday or even Friday. A small meeting was under way in my room, and Shaktidas as always was taking the lead on various projects such as how to imitate lizards in the best way. 'Do a clucky sound, man, chluck, chluck, but not like chigen,' he was saying, sitting straight-backed and very serious. The topic was brought up because Nooby being an ant was worried about lizard movements, which according to him were increasing uncharacteristically for this time of the year. How better to chase away lizards than in their own language? Frauntfraunty was convinced he knew how to say 'go away and never come back' in lizard language. And so it went back and forth between Broom and Frauntfraunty and neither gave in. Broom's irritation was growing every second and finally when he couldn't argue any longer, he turned to Nooby to ask for a final decision. Where was Nooby? He was nowhere to be seen. Not in the cupboard either. Shaktidas grew concerned and said, 'He is make many fight and all, sir, very strange.' I nodded and agreed. He had been unusually feisty and absent alternatively. Usually he was back in a few minutes so we decided to wait, and meanwhile practise the spider stare, the only known way one could chase away those eight-legged beasts. But suddenly BringOverMarty began to cry and say a sad poem, 'The one who is gone, is never coming back, the one who is gone, is likely in a sack, heading to the deathly kingdom, from where we all come, and then return, we are all doomed . . .' In the usual way, his rhyme began to collapse towards the end, and Broom comforted him with a whiskery arm around his small shoulders. 'Sorry, sir,' he said finally, 'Emotions are unstable these days, one day angry, one day scared, forgive me, sir, for I am weak . . .' I cut him short and patted his head and we were all quiet. But Nooby never came back.

We adjusted quite soon, but that emptiness when a friend goes away is never filled. All meetings thereon had a voice missing and sometimes we found ourselves waiting a little too long, as if unconsciously we still waited for Nooby to say something, something silly and dirty like he always did. With a lump in my throat it was always I who said, 'OK, let's move on', and I would look sadly at Nooby's cupboard and wonder what happened to my strange little ant friend.

Over time all my friends disappeared, one by one, into the darkness of the universe, without saying a word about their departure. Only Shaktidas, the wise one, hinted at it one night as we lay in bed. 'Ib, you're grown up now. You'll have to do things on your own.' 'Why, Broom?' I asked. 'Adults need help, too.' 'Yes, from other adults you know. Not from small people like us.'

'But I like you guys,' I said. He smiled and looked around helplessly.

'You have us now, and we won't go anywhere if we can help it. But the world is a dark and dangerous place, and I don't think we can last for long outside this room. Besides, things aren't in our control.'

'I'll protect you guys, I promise.'

Broom laughed. 'Who knows, maybe you'll be better off without me. The world is dark and dangerous . . .'

It was the first time Shaktidas had spoken so clearly.

In the morning he was gone and soon I realized that they were nothing more than figments of my loneliness, manifested as friends, but that was much later, when I was truly grown up.

It was lonely without them, but I found I went outside more often now that I had no meetings to attend, no discussions to moderate. I missed Shaktidas's wisdom, Nooby's bad language, BringOverMarty's songs and Frauntfraunty's devotion, yet I saw more of the world, and learnt to see things differently, as a loner, and digest them into my mind. There was no one to cry to, no one to complain to, and this worked out well.

24

TWO

It is difficult to put a man into words. I have known many men, and some women, and some kids too; but it is difficult to put them into these tiny squiggly forms, whatever shapes you use. And it gets worse as the men become more men, greater larger men, deeper men with intense eyes and great manifestos and jurisdictions, with slanting opinions and strong ideas.

One such man was my grandfather; a small in size man but who carried himself with great height, bald to a degree of polish rarely seen on scalp.

Were you wondering how did we survive? With money, with food? It was Grandfather who provided for us, after Appoos lost his power of earning, and he made it felt that he was the provider, constantly. I haven't mentioned him because somewhere I don't want to, and yet I need to, because he was always there, like a background of dark clouds, scary, but the soil needed the rain and so you learn to live with that fear.

He—Ajju, I called him—was not a reasonable man, and one could not put to bed anything with reason. Instead, to conclude a discussion or argument with this person, my grandfather (although arguments with him were rare, owing to the force of his character that somehow cut down feelings or urges of rebellion within the minds of his opponents), the wait had to be made for *him* to end the topic. He would typically perform this by tone rather than content: The weight of it, combined with the unspoken threat of stiffness and silence, quiet anger, unspeakable disappointment at anyone who maintained the opposing position, disgust, and a violent (by understatement) rise of his upper lip, would essentially end words and further discussion. It was as if disagreeing with him was unacceptable and that was that. An exclusive club existed at whose jokes Ajju laughed and for nobody else, but this was too, a strange kind of laughter, nothing in it suggesting enjoyment or good humour, rather a kind of approval. So it was that look of 'I know' that was most frequent on his round, clean-shaven face and it very often crept up to his turtle-shell bald head. It was the only scalp I have seen that seemed to know you were looking at it, and approved of this.

When Appoos lost his 'sensibility' and was no longer a respectable constituent of this so-called structured but actually amorphous, this so-called amorphous but actually rigid, thing called society, Ajju began visiting more often, in his rigid army way, and would often call four days in advance, though he lived only an hour away. The phone, a hunky, maroon frog-like thing, screamed like a banshee and

Amma in the kitchen, her back to me, would instruct me with her hand to answer it. Plans were barked through from the other end: Too quickly I was required to remember but I did, knowing and thinking forward to the consequences of error. And in his presence, errors were seldom made: Though this said more of minimum risk rather than maximum performance.

When Ajju arrived, Amma was always inside her room so she wouldn't have to face his at-once commanding manner, about cleanliness and how shoe racks ought to be arranged, and I was the little stick on which the torrent of his forceful manner would crash down. He was always irritated and annoyed and I don't know what I ever did, though I know that it was never what I did, but somehow, was made to feel like it was.

Grandfather had a farm an hour from the city. From the gentle hill beside the house, I saw the shadows of clouds for the first time, as they passed slowly across the green patchwork plain, spangling green farms and barren earth in amorphous patches of light and charcoal shade. The chiaroscuro of this scene in my mind is much clearer and the shadows much sharper perhaps than when I witnessed it and I remember the silhouette of Appoos's face against that wide land despite him never coming up that hill. Ajju was the only one who came up the hill because Amma was afraid of leopards. 'Many killings have been reported,' she said. An adult was required for even this little adventure that I wished to have. In a discussion, it was decided that Appoos could not protect a child from a predator and by

27

default then it was decided Grandfather would be the one. When we reached the top, he held me by the shoulder and pretended to give me instructions but it was clear that he needed to lean on something. I said, 'Don't worry, Ajju. You sit down. I won't go far. And I won't tell Amma that you left me alone.' He bristled but his physical exertion had dissolved his pride and he nodded breathlessly. I had left Shaktidas and the others down below. I stood alone, looking through the dry lantana and feeling the crackling wind on my skin. The forest was on the right; a deep green line that curved gently from my hill to the common horizon. I began to walk, leaving Ajju's bent grey figure behind and rounding a natural hedge of lantana and old gnarled trees that reminded me of old men. How nice it would be, I thought, to become a tree when you die, instead of just dying? And it was this thought of death that occupied my mind while my eyes were fixed and fascinated by nature and its reticent expression, the awesome silence from human voices and the occasional and remote bark of a deer or the whistling of a winged schoolboy. Finding myself at the edge of the hill (beyond was the land), I sat on a grey and rust outcrop of cold rocks.

Presently, a rustling became apparent from the lantana, and turning, I saw the yellow dangerous eyes of a leopard, set in a mottled and strong head, low by the ground. By the sides of his head, haunches rose—rippled and tight strung—and yet he only sat still, his eyes in a constant attentive anger, fixed on the slight form of a confused bipedal creature, and he wondered I think, what I was doing there. Enchanted out of fear and caution I rose, and walked a few steps closer and he scuttled backwards further into the bushes, into the shadows, till he was only spots of yellow in an otherwise green and brown mass with only his eyes that gave away the nature of this tangled beast to be more than just branch and twig. He watched me for a while longer, then slunk away and the shadows of the thin branches and little leaves on his golden-yellow fur melded with the dark of his spots, and he moved stealthily, as those dancing shadows flowed away, over and against the direction of his movement, till they dropped silently off his smooth back. Then there was nothing but the howling of the wind. I had suddenly begun to feel cold and noticed the attention of the hair on my arms. Later that night, we heard him once, as we sat around the empty fireplace and Amma looked suddenly at the bolts and clutched the torch that she always kept close. Of course I never told them, despite it being the most exciting thing I had ever experienced.

* * *

Grandfather was simple in a strange way, in the way that a monstrous creature is perhaps simple. Killer Croc terrorizing the sewers of New York City was simple; all he wanted to do was kill people, end Batman, perhaps motivated by some sense of revenge, but is it that simple to say, 'such and such is my one motivation'? Hence, the monster can be seen as a simple creature, whereas us good people are complicated creatures, lost and confused among the wreckage of this modern life. Like that, Grandfather had simple motives: To be in control, to be wise, to be the one in the room who knows, to be the teller of the joke, the teller of the one story of the evening. One can think of this force in his attitude as a result of a violently random life, full of death and travel. But who are we to say what caused this or that? He had a great respect for the law, for the police, for the nation, and unconsciously hated the loser in every situation. For him the new India was industry and money and he didn't have time, he said, for the whimpering of locals who didn't want a factory here or a mine there. He was a great advocate of the greater good. Of course, all this was beyond me at that time, and for me all he was, was a man who ordered mother around rudely.

In the evenings, when he visited, Ajju sat in his favourite cane chair on a faded red cushion, while everyone else scurried around for dinner and for this and that. He had a way of conveying that he was waiting for things even without saying anything. When his evening scotch arrived on a small tray with a bowl of ice, he helped himself with an absent-minded approval and I remember Amma hurrying away, relieved that he didn't scold her about the glass being dirty or the drops of whiskey on the tray. Sometimes, quite rarely, he spoke to me and it was always some advice and never a question, and to this day I keep in mind that the ones who don't ask you questions, they're the ones who probably should be asking you questions because you're wiser than they are. But he used to say, 'Ib, young man, the country is in a great big mess, and these bloody pacifists want to shut down the army. They are out of touch. Out of touch.' His words possessed some strange wind that made one nod, a subtle but unmistakable pressure at the back of the neck that made me move my head. And he would say, 'People who weren't in the army have no idea about life. Go to the frontline, then you'll see. They ought to take young men like you there to see the reality that the cities hide.' But mostly there was only a tense silence, as everyone waited for Grandfather to say something.

Once in the late 1990s, one evening, Ajju was more silent, less disapproving. He had his drink, of course, once the guy in the mosque was done screaming, but there was less enjoyment and pleasure and instead some kind of relief as if he had had a rough day. Now, it must be said that my grandfather never had a rough day, such was his handle on things, the way he would catch the morning by the scruff of its neck and wring it till a purposeful, statured, sunshine bled through every pore of his body. It was unusual, thus, to see him slightly beaten down, as if the morning had shunned him a little, ignored his daily routine and went about things saying, 'Hey, everyone's having a bummer, dude, live with it,' or something else with that customary callousness with which the weather and time go about things. I watched as he sat there quietly, and this quietness was different from the usual tense silence. Mom was worried: When someone you fear is being nice—or less scary—you feel even worse than normal, because you wonder what will set them off. This difference in their behaviour makes them unpredictable. She stood at the

31

kitchen door biting her nails until she couldn't take it any more and went to her father and crouched by his chair. 'Papa, do you want something?' she asked quietly. He moved the paper so it covered his face and said a little too loudly, 'No, nothing, ma, nothing.' It was all very strange. Was Ajju actually feeling sad? It was too much for my little mind, and so after a large glass of yellow milk, I went upstairs feeling exceptionally tired (which is perhaps why I remember this incident with such clarity).

I tried to figure him out that night as I lay in bed listening to the howls and barks of dogs. Maybe he was reminded of his friends who died in the mountains, high up in the snowy Himalayas. What creatures lived in the Himalayas? I knew nothing.

The next day, he was back to normal, stern, irritated, and we were all a little relieved. It was only a couple of months after that, one morning, when Amma, looking through some old pictures said, 'Ib, you remember Mammu? See, this was the day they met in Delhi. They were together for forty-two years, baba. Imagine that! Forty-two years.' Her voice trailed off into a sad silence and she looked up from the photographs and into some memories in the distance. So it wasn't death that made Ajju sad, I thought, but some sad forgotten memory of him being happy. And perhaps it was this memory of happiness that made Ajju most sad, sadder than anything else.

THREE

Earlier I asked, 'Where must I begin?' Now I ask 'Why?' There's no good reason, just an urge to say things, to describe things, to show some angles, and some light glinting off them, or some unexpected shadows where none should be.

33

And all this is nothing if not a description of my shape. I am thin, certainly, quite capable of not being seen, yet not so capable that I can disappear when required or large and looming when that is the need.

And it must be said that I was perhaps one of these strangely shaped creatures for whom time and space do not make much time or space, and this has left me irregular and broken and bent. While everyone around seemed smooth and aerodynamic (except my family), I felt always as if the winds of life, of the future, or the past were not so agreeable as they flowed around. But I have spoken too much already of matters greater than myself and the world around; perhaps that is for the end.

It strikes me now: Everything Ajju told me, I did the opposite. It was as if adulthood was something he had sparked in me, like water sparks a flower, and my childhood, small and weak anyway, disappeared like the tips of burning cigarettes. There was nothing I could do: Man came into me like darkness comes into the evening, despite some sun, and however much you want a few more minutes of daylight, it just comes. You can be clever and go inside, put on the lights, performing in a few steps and an action what man has done to nature. But of course, one needs to know where the switches are, the operation of them. This was knowledge I had not come upon yet. Only when we are old do we know why being young is nice. We are all children, if only for a brief moment, and spend the rest of our lives trying to be children again: In those papery light moments near a moon, near a tree by a river or a funny moment in a film. Now where have all the children gone? What happened in that middle section? So it was that I became a man without really trying, and found that it was something that had happened to me rather than something I did. And like darkness that makes the evening opaque, that makes air thick, Man-ness grew inside and made me opaque. Then I was an opaque man before the age of fourteen and never again was delicate or nice.

I enjoyed this opaqueness at first: It filled me with a tough cement, with a hard currency to trade with against the problems of life. Appoos didn't bother me any more, I found, and Amma less so. And Foreign Uncle—it had been years since I had seen him—was soon a flickering memory.

But soon, feeling strong at first, this thickness all went to my skin, leaving my insides empty. This emptiness I found later was a side-effect: this emptiness or an unjustified fullness that leads eventually to more emptiness. Shoulders and shoulders, thousands more, empty and opaque make up a city. No wonder they say cities are empty. And it was also around this time that I began to realize that I was smarter than all the adults I had known: this was the last straw of childhood, and it broke the small camel's back.

As I grew, strange things happened, to my body, to the world. Planes hit buildings in America and thousands died. After that everyone was afraid of everything all the time. Things got stricter, I heard, everywhere and Muslims were suspects. Appoos was a Muslim. Would he fly a plane into a building? Was he a different Muslim from other Muslims? In school, they said, 'Ib, you're a Muslim because your father is a Muslim.' And I said, 'No, I don't pray to Allah, how can I be Muslim?'

'Who do you pray to?' asked one of the big boys, whose face was oily.

'God.'

'Which god?'

'I don't know.'

'What do you say? How do you pray?'

'I say, 'Please, god, make my parents live forever.''

'Then you're Christian, I think,' said the big boy. The others nodded. But another big boy, a gentler one, who smiled at me sometimes said, 'But you weren't born a Christian, so how can you be a Christian?'

'Isn't your mother Hindu?' asked another boy. I nodded.

There was a small discussion. Finally oily big boy put his hands up for silence. 'Only god knows what you are,' he said. 'Because when you pray, if you say god, then you're praying to Christian god; if you say Allah, you're praying to Allah; and Hindu, if you say Ram or Ganesha. But if you say god and in your mind you're saying Allah, then you're Muslim. And if you're born Muslim, then that is what you are. Only god knows.'

'Which god?' asked a meek fellow looking around confused.

'All god is one,' said someone from the back.

And so discussions like this were carried out often when my religion was brought into question. But because of this spiritual bipartisanship, I was never suspected of being a terrorist. And yet the bigger questions sometimes came to me at night and I would toss and turn thinking— who were these Muslims who wanted to kill people? And why do some Muslims not kill people? And why do some non-Muslims kill people? And why do some non-Muslims not kill people? The world was a scary and confusing place.

There was another Muslim boy in class who wore a skullcap sometimes, on Fridays and holy days. He was always quiet and someone said that his mother wore a black burqa and nobody knew what she looked like. 'What about the father?' I asked Biju, who knew everything.

'The father wears shirt and pant only,' Biju said.

'Why?'

'Muslim women wear like that only, Ib. It's to protect the women from men who stare.'

'Can she remove it if she wants to?'

'Don't question all these things, Ib. Shameem ma'am might be offended,' he said softly.

So the Muslim women had two layers around them that made them invisible. One was the black cloth, the other, a dark taboo of speaking about it lest it offends someone. How hot they must feel, I thought to myself, with these two insulated layers keeping them hidden from the outside world.

I declared to everyone the next day that I was not of any religion, because everything about it was beginning to irritate me. You could ask questions, but as soon as the question began to hurt or poke or pinch or tickle, no more questions (and what is the point of questions that don't sting?). Ma was thrilled because she too wasn't very religious now after Appoos went mad, and considered it a waste of time and money. 'If every priest became a gardener, and every temple goer went for a jog instead, the world would be a much better place,' she said, when I told her. She made me my favourite caramel pudding that night.

'Don't mention it to Ajju,' she said over dinner.

But I found that apparently religious people weren't happy just being religious. They wanted everyone else to be religious too. This I found one morning when I reached class and the Muslim boy whose mother was covered in a black cloth came to me and pushed my books on the floor.

'You are *murtid*,' he said, spitting the word out like venom. 'Shame on your family, shame on you.'

I didn't understand what he said. But I could see on his face that it was something terrible. Never in my life, to this day, have I seen the face of a child so grotesque and hateful. A few others watched, waiting for a fight, but he went back to his desk and began to read. Every now and then he glanced towards me with hate and fear. I picked up the books and sat down, and realized my hands were shaking.

When I went home I asked Amma what he had meant. She was upset and said she would call the principal. 'Ma, please don't,' I pleaded, 'it'll make things worse.'

She didn't say anything and sat slowly.

'What is it, Ma? What did he mean?'

'It means apostate, someone who leaves Islam.'

'But I was never Muslim,' I said.

She sighed. 'Religion and government,' she said finally, 'nothing is straightforward in these two things.'

'I don't understand, Ma.'

'Neither do I.' She laughed sadly and looked towards the room in which Appoos slept.

'Even your father isn't Muslim,' she said. 'He was an atheist before he . . . you know what.'

I nodded and felt for the first time pride.

'Why didn't you tell me, Ma?'

'Why, Ib? Are you an atheist?' she asked, and in her voice was surprise and then gentle mocking.

'I don't know,' I said, 'but religion is the worst. I'm not any religion.'

'Good, babu, religion only leads to suffering. It's a horrible thing.'

She had made fried idlis and I ate in silence thinking of what Appoos would have been like if he was normal.

* * *

There was a great deal to wonder about, about the world. My small mind felt bulged and swollen sometimes when I came across some amazing facts about the universe. No god would have created such a large wasteland of blackness and non-living things. It was larger by a billion times what the holy books said. But not only in the sky, in the earth and in the soul. There was too much to know, too much to unknow, too much that could not be known, at least not in my lifetime. Where did worms go? What were the birds thinking? Why do dogs serve so faithfully? Why are we here?

These things kept me awake at night because it all seemed too fickle, so coincidental, so precarious. But man was his own safekeeper, his own guardian. Otherwise the universe would have killed us a long time ago. So in man must we believe and give strength to the institutions of man, and not god. The mind of man had made so much, and yet everyone talked only of how much he had unmade.

This troubled me in school. We were constantly told how bad man was and yet nobody looked around them and saw the wonders. Without us we wouldn't be here. One day in class someone said, 'We should wipe ourselves out with a nuclear bomb,' and he didn't realize

39

Ib's Endless Search for Satisfaction

that that would mean he would be dead and couldn't see the benefits. The small-minded were often like that. They reacted with great passion and with a sense of justice, but little else and no thinking. This was harmful in the long run. These people let their ideas and convictions shape reality rather than the other way around, and by this they were deluded and harmful. The world was full of them, and I would see one every day in the paper, or in school, on TV. But people admired them because they had the most seductive ideas that appealed to fickle-minded humans, and made them feel good. Very few had the strength to see things as they were because things as they were didn't let you sleep.

One such person was Sanjeet, the senior boy who smiled at me. He was tall and had a large nose, which he said came from Afghanistan. He spoke to me often, but not for long. He would say 'hi' or 'how are you?', things like that and pass by in the corridor. This was rare because seniors rarely said hi to the juniors, whom they considered bugs and insects unworthy of their time.

But Sanjeet was a different sort. He walked separately and not in a group and his head was always turned slightly down, as if he was thinking sadly about something while the others near him were laughing and screaming and jumping about. He was quieter too, and rarely spoke in assembly when questions were asked. I was told he was from a rich family from some huge city, but he didn't show it. One day we met in the garden. He was examining a spiderweb that was stretched between the leaves of a water lily like a delicate silk rainbow. The spider squatted in the middle waiting; patient and sinister. Sanjeet crouched on the lip of the pond. I sat next to him and he said 'hi' like he usually did and went back to observing.

'Which is that spider?' I asked.

'Common garden spider,' he said, and began to explain some facts about them; their strengths, their interests— the males were smaller than the females, who ate them after mating. 'They are a unique species, spiders, because of this.'

I sniggered when he said mate and he laughed too. These were sensitive, forbidden topics.

'Do you like animals?' he asked. I nodded. He began to talk more about pond ecosystems. He was doing a project about it, he said. Soon a bell rang and he got up. 'Take care of the spider, Ib,' he said, 'the birds come sometimes.'

I nodded determinedly and took my position by the web. Nothing would get the spider while I was there.

In the evening I was still there when Sanjeet came back. 'You're still here?' he exclaimed. He was with four boys and a girl. He began to tell them how I had protected the spider for four hours. The boys said 'cool, man' and 'that's cool, bro', and began to talk among themselves of something the teacher said in class, but the girl smiled and pushed her dark hair behind her ear. 'Which class are you in?' she asked gently, and her voice was smooth and deep. 'Seventh,' I mumbled. She seemed to see straight through my face into my mind, and my face began to turn red. The girl giggled and looked at Sanjeet who was smiling.

41

'Thanks, Ib,' he said, 'she'll be fine at night.' I got up and mumbled something and ran till my legs began to hurt.

* * *

Sports were meant to be fun, but I never had fun. The hardness of them, the violence, the speed: these things were uncomfortable to me, and didn't suit my small body. And the competition, the winning attitude, was something I could never kindle within myself. Some boys were really up and running for football or cricket. But I would walk slowly, reluctantly, hoping that something would happen— rain, hail, snow, tornado, a death in the family, a fracture— anything that would pull me away from the terror of dust and flying balls, and big guys who shouted.

But mostly none of these things happened and it was compulsory to play a sport in the evening, even if sport to you was not really a sport but a chore that hurt the next day. Sport was the benchmark, by which you were known in a school like that, and nobody remembered the boy who didn't play a sport.

And so I would trudge to the field, and be the last to be picked, and the captain who picked me always looked around to see if he'd missed anyone. When the game began, I would run about like a mad hen, making up for lack of skill, vision, ambition, competition by sheer speed, so nobody thought I wasn't doing anything. Mostly this worked out, but the ball sometimes, despite the wishes of everyone on my team, would come hurtling towards me out of the dust. It was a hard large ball and stung my legs. I would hear a voice through the clouds of dust (or the clouds in my head) say, 'Pass, pass, pass, here.' And another voice, 'Pass the ball, Ib, PASS!' But it was too late. I would be staggering around, trying to kick the ball that was already in someone else's possession, running through the dust towards our goal. And someone else, running past me, towards the attacker threatening our goal, would say, 'Just pass the ball, Ib, that's all.'

This lack of presence of mind was my trademark in these games. But when the ball was still, I wasn't too bad and could think about what to do with it. Often, I would take corners because of this luxury of time and thought that they provided. Yet, this was a skill not valuable enough for me to be picked enthusiastically.

This applied in other aspects of life as well. When there was time to think, I was pretty good, but street smartness wasn't my talent. Girls were all about street smartness; the ones who could whip a line out, swish and dance, were the ones the girls liked, and the quiet ones, who barely spoke, were thought to be losers. In the corridors when a pretty girl passed I always panicked and never even looked towards her face, and don't know to this day if one of them smiled at me, or frowned. The game of young love was all about smartness and surface things, and there was no room for time and space. Not that the girls would have lined up if I was street smart. Even with a good head about me, I was still a small, unsportsmanlike, quiet loser and this never worked to my advantage.

Later my face grew OK, straightened out, filled in. After college I was suddenly introduced to the thrilling, confusing and terrifying phenomena of attention from girls, but in school, I was probably invisible to them.

And when this wasn't the case, for example, by some strange twist of fate, a girl did look at me, a pretty girl, my face burnt and turned red, and courage failed me. Every time this happened, it weakened my confidence until by the time school was over, I was terrified of pretty girls, and avoided them like a sexy plague.

Between classes I hung out with a few others, odd fellows like myself, who were quiet and skirted around happenings. A plump boy—dark and oily faced—who was constantly pulling his trousers up, whose name I cannot remember, had many questions about girls and boobs and vaginas, and I never had any answers. The few who did know never hung around with us.

The plump boy, troubled constantly and frowning, tried many times to flip to the 'vagina' section in the Encyclopaedia Britannica but he was always too nervous and all he could do was catch a glimpse of a technical drawing of one, flower-like, but strangely flat and unappealing. He complained to us that it looked boring and asked himself what the big deal was and why everyone was running around behind girls when all they had was that thing. Sanjeet helped us out when he could but Sanjeet was an honourable sort and it was tricky bringing up these subjects with him. Yet some desperation, perhaps biological, or something deeper, pushed me one day while we were going back home, by the park and without thinking I stopped in front of him and asked him, 'What is sex?

44

Is it vagina?' He laughed and looked embarrassed and pushed me aside. But encouraged by his laugh I persisted and finally he explained the process and it was the worst thing I'd ever heard in my life. I shuddered and promised him that I would never think about girls again. 'No wonder I can't talk to girls,' I said as he dropped me near my house. 'They're so disgusting.'

'Yeah, right,' he said smiling. 'So why did you run from Simran that day near the pond?'

'I felt so disgusted, that's why.'

He laughed again and patted my shoulder and said bye.

But they were strange, girls, and confusing, and I found I was constantly thinking about their faces and bodies, even though they were so disgusting and I didn't want to go anywhere near them and yet when I saw them I felt scared and embarrassed and conscious as if it mattered a lot what they thought of me.

I wanted to explain to that plump boy the whole sex thing and hoped he would join me in thinking it was sick and gross but when I found him one afternoon he said he had looked on the Internet and it felt good to see women and men having sex. The concept made me shudder again.

'Check the Internet, Ib,' he whispered, 'It's amazing to see.'

The Internet? I had no way of checking it because we didn't even own a computer, and technology wasn't welcome in my mother's house. 'It's too much of everything,' she said, when I asked her about the Internet.

'But everyone has it, Ma,' I pleaded.

She turned around and said firmly, 'Not under my roof. If you want, go the cyber cafe or wherever you young people go to waste time these days but not here.'

What a strange day it was as I made my way to the internet cafe full of adult men who looked at me suspiciously as if I was doing something wrong. Inside the room, it was hot and smelled sour like a sweaty T-shirt.

'How old are you?' asked the man at the counter. I told him and he shrugged and pointed me towards the far cubicle.

'You know how to use?' he asked mockingly. I shook my head.

He took the mouse in his hand and pushed an icon on the screen.

'This is web browser. In this you can find websites.'

I thanked him and he left grumbling.

Where would I find sex? I followed his instructions and typed in the bar on top of the screen a single word—'sex'—and my heart thumping, I waited.

It took a while but finally the screen began to fill up with words and pictures. 'What is sex?' 'How to prevent sexually transmitted diseases?' And right at the bottom of the page, below all the knowledge and the science, there was a short, blue sentence claiming, 'Hottest sex videos'. Nervously, looking around to see if anyone was watching, I clicked and suddenly the screen filled up full of photographs of naked men and women in various positions, like nude acrobats, doing impossible things with their legs and faces.

It was a strange feeling and I felt it in places that till then had never felt much. Transfixed, I clicked through, clicking and clicking, more and more photographs of beautiful women with large breasts, legs wide open, faces in expressions of ecstasy, moaning and panting and biting and licking. And as I stared at the screen, a pressure grew inside me, growing and growing as I delved deeper and deeper into that strange, naked world, and finally a short video began to play: a woman's face as a man pushed his huge penis (how could it grow that huge and what kind of underwear would you need?) into her vagina, eyes rolled up into her sockets in deep and infinite pleasure and suddenly the pressure released and something down in my pants exploded and the front of my pants were wet. It wasn't urine because there wasn't enough and there was no smell and I never felt such a deep sense of satisfaction after pissing—and my pants weren't even *that* wet. So, confused, I quickly paid and left, feeling exhausted and elated at the same time.

Later I learnt about things, the fluids and pressures involved, the plumbing that made children, and I looked back at that incident with embarrassment and relief— embarrassment about how easily I was brought to the edge and relief that nobody had walked in and caught me watching pornography.

That was the beginning. After that my dreams were filled to the brim with women's bodies; the fluids, the violence of sex, their orgasming faces and for years I thought about nothing else.

* * *

That year, there was a storm one evening, and everyone was caught in class and couldn't go back home because storms were rare there and nobody knew what to do. Ranjit's father came in a huge Mercedes and drove off with a few boys. The sky was dark with clouds and the lights were growing dim, flickering, the sun and the few artificial ones that lined the street outside. Anjali, a girl who lived near my house, stood shivering near the door because she was caught in the rain and had to run back inside. 'How are you going home?' she asked me. I shrugged and kept looking out into the hard rain. Finally she came and stood next to me. 'We can call an auto,' she said. Awkward as I was, I said OK, and she went inside the classroom to make a call from the teacher's phone. She was back in a few minutes, her hair undone, and I noticed her breasts under the wet shirt. 'He's coming in a few minutes.' She began to throw her hair about with her hands, slapping it on her back, and with every swish, her scent, mixed with the wetness of rain, rushed over my face.

We waited and waited. Now there was nobody there but us and Ms Sheila who sat inside at her desk, waiting for us to leave. Finally she couldn't take it any more and came rushing to the door. 'Anjali, I'm leaving, sweety,' she said, opening out her umbrella and speeding past us. 'Lock the door when you go.' We watched as her red umbrella disappeared into the thick rain lit by a yellow street lamp.

'Maybe we should walk back,' she said after a while. 'It's not so bad any more.'

I agreed. We began to walk. There was a light rain, and the distant sound of thunder. Puddles and streams covered the road, and it was impossible to keep one's feet dry.

Soon she turned towards me as we walked and asked, 'Why are you so quiet, Ib? It's not normal.'

I laughed and shrugged. 'I don't know what to say,' I said.

'Anything. It's better than this weird silence.'

'I don't find it weird at all. I like listening to the rain. It muffles the other dirty city sounds.'

She listened for a moment and agreed.

We walked in silence but soon she turned again as we went past a bright building with a large neon red sign that said City Market.

'What do your parents do?' she asked.

It had been a long time since anyone had asked me that question and I had lost the touch to answer cleverly with artifice and so spoke plainly.

'My father is schizophrenic, and my mother takes care of him,' I said.

'Oh shit,' she said. 'I didn't know.'

'It's fine. Nobody knows really.'

She was quiet for the rest of the walk, afraid perhaps of asking an awkward question. Awkwardness for some people is the greatest evil.

When we reached her house she hugged me and thanked me. 'I'll see you tomorrow at school,' she said. I waved when she was at her door and when she was inside began to walk, now at a much quicker pace, my mind occupied as usual by fantasies of what might have happened if I had the courage to hold her hand as we crossed the wet roads, her breasts under her wet shirt, her thick hair, her skin the colour of a dark afternoon.

* * *

Those days when the moon grew full and swelled up like an ivory balloon and the nights were molten silver, I would sneak out at midnight and meet some of the boys. They were bored too at night, because when the days are regular and plain, with no pops or cracks, the nights become the time to explore and feel something. Nights were always mysterious and lit by the deep orange of old street lamps. We met in a few different places prearranged by one of the big boys, and his word was final, generally, unless there was valid reason to be otherwise. One night was the bridge, one night the park by the city centre, all quite close to our homes and quite safe, or so we thought. Safety isn't always teenage boys' top priority, and we were more concerned with not being seen by the police rather than by the criminal element.

We were under the bridge one night and drinking beer from cans that one of the big boys had brought. Everyone was grinning nervously at each other and laughing. Sanjeet was quiet as he usually was and stood sentry while we stood in a loose circle passing cans amongst ourselves. Sanjeet didn't want to drink because he was nervous and didn't like losing control.

We weren't the only ones under the bridge. A few beggars and tramps moved about slowly mumbling, clattering their sacks of bottles and cans. One old man waited for us to finish our beer so he could collect his livelihood. He stood in the dark, where the light couldn't reach him and watched us attentively. When another beggar approached, he threw a pebble and shouted something till the other one shuffled away. Rohit laughed and I thought it was quite a cruel thing to laugh in the face of a miserable man. Sanjeet seemed annoyed too and frowned at Rohit who paid no attention. The other boys were involved in some talk of football and movies. John, a tall, dark fellow, was talking about a club called Manchester United; and the others were confused because here there were countries and apparently in Europe there were clubs. 'No, man,' he said, 'there are countries there too. But they play football in clubs. Like there is Manchester United, Chelsea, Liverpool. And in Spain there is Barcelona, Real Madrid. I'm a Liverpool supporter.' He smiled proudly and showed everyone his red T-shirt that said the name of some player, Gerry, or some such.

Rohit was done with his beer and threw it down on the ground. The beggar shuffled out from the shadows, on his face a curious mix of gratitude and hate. Why did he have to throw it down? Everyone knew the beggar was waiting for the can. A decent person would have given it to him. Rohit said, 'Filthy fuck, these beggars.' 'Go get a job,' he shouted at the beggar's bent, grimy back. Sanjeet turned suddenly. 'Stop that,' he said, and his face was red in the dark of the night and his eyes glistened with anger and fear. Rohit was a big guy after all and Sanjeet was never into fights. But Rohit mumbled something and

51

was quiet. All conversation had stopped and everyone looked at each other and sighed. It was getting as if somebody had diverted a stream of cold wind into the space beneath the bridge. 'Shall we go?' asked John, his fingers fiddling with an empty can. It was late and everyone agreed. Rohit was still mumbling and avoided Sanjeet as best he could. On our way back there was a policeman hitting a beggar with his cane. Rohit was about to say something but decided against it. The group split and there was only Sanjeet and me for the last stretch. He walked with his hands clasped behind his back like an old man. 'I hate that Rohit,' he said at last, as we turned into our street. He turned to me. 'Don't go hang out with that guy, OK?' I nodded and he punched me gently in the shoulder. 'See you at school.' I entered the garden over the wall, silently, and he stood under the street light until I was inside. From the window I watched as he made sure nobody was around. Then he turned and went home.

The next day at school, Rohit was not apologetic or the least remorseful. Perhaps he was drunk but everyone said that was not possible because he drank quite often and one can of beer was like juice to him. I wondered how that would feel, to drink every day, and it scared me, because I too, liked being in control.

'He's just a bad guy,' said Trishul, who was with us the previous night. 'I can see it in his eyes.'

Manu said his father was a politician and was known in these parts to be a violent goonda who grabbed land, threw people off roofs. 'He's killed three people,' he added in a whisper. However old we became, there was still someone to scare us. A few years earlier it was ghosts. At lunch in the cacophony of the dining hall, we discussed the evils of the Indian system; the judges were paid, the cops were evil, the politicians filthy with corruption. It was almost as if the worst of the worst became the ones who were meant to be the best of the best. 'Nothing works in this country without bribes,' said Pradeep, whose father owned a huge farm somewhere in the hills. He nodded sadly and ate his vegetable. Everyone agreed, of course. And everyone was a sceptic soon, and everyone hated the system, and everyone hated the rules because the rules came from the system. 'What's the point of paying taxes?' asked someone else. There was no point.

I looked around the table and saw citizens who were already fed up, already hateful, already tired. How could India awake when she was already dead?

'Anarchism is the only way,' said Vipul with grim confidence.

'Anar-what?'

'Anar is a fruit.'

'Not that anar. Anarchism. No system of government is good for the people.'

'Ya, man, that sounds correct,' said Manu, 'I think I'll be a anarchismist.'

'Anarchist,' said Vipul, but Manu was already talking about something else and Vipul went back to eating his rice and dal.

* * *

When school finished, everyone had great plans and no doubts. But I had no plans and only doubts. Suddenly I had to decide things instead of being pushed here and there and told to do things. But I had no idea where I wanted to go, what I wanted to do. I had no great interests, no passions, no guiding principles. I was a lost boy suddenly becoming hairy.

On the last day, everyone stood in groups discussing their futures: colleges, universities, countries, tests of various kinds, and I wandered around pretending to be busy and pretending to know what they were talking about. The teachers passed by patting me on the back: Only they knew how hopeless I was, because only they had seen my scores. To the others I was a smart guy because I spoke smart. The maths teacher, a smelly, ratty man who was always on time, travelled from group to group speaking words of encouragement and congratulations, and when he saw me, he pretended that he had a meeting and left. He had nothing to say to me because saying hopeless things was not permitted in these circumstances of celebration and melancholy.

I waved goodbye to my few friends. We hugged and shook hands. 'We'll keep in touch,' said someone. I nodded and left by the back door, and the plants by the rear path said, 'Another wasteful recruit. They always leave through the back door.'

PART 2

FOUR

Once school ended there was a buzz in the house as though something exciting was about to happen, but this feeling was rooted in wishful thinking and the dreams of my mother rather than in anything real. Once school ended there were supposed to be some things happening in and around your life—freedom and college, drinking and coming home late. But if you stayed at home, like I did, nobody came into your home and took you by the hand and led you out into the world. You had to do this yourself and this somehow I wasn't taught, and was taught instead that the world was a wonderful place full of happiness and helpful people, but in truth it was a cruel and rude place and nobody looked twice if you fell from your cycle and nobody helped you up.

But I still stayed at home, even though I understood that the hand-holding of school was over, and the hands were all cold and unheld, and the warmth of holding hands was replaced by the callouses of trying to take a hold of life. That was the beginning of an adult struggle.

But soon Appoos began to get on my nerves and mother's passivity was even worse and these two things drove me out of the house.

I began to wander here and there and in wandering I found a freedom that I enjoyed very much, a kind of freedom for which one didn't really have to do anything or work very hard. All you had to do was get out of the house, leaving mental illness behind, and walk around and nothing mattered; yet you saw a lot, and smelt a lot. There was a lot to learn from the smelly world outside.

Some days I would walk past the school and see the kids—different actors in the same roles in that endless play—and try spotting the ones who were playing me; the losers, the low-energy misfits, the fringe-nibblers. They were always there—those border skirters, those edge shufflers—looking scared and trying to slip out before the teachers saw them or their friends noticed.

By the school there was a lake which was out of bounds when we were students, and because of this it became a place that everyone wanted to go urgently. For a month or so after passing out of that school the students made it a point to visit that lake, and since it was within the line of sight of the staff building, they thought that the teachers could see them and that they would curse and raise their fists at the window. But they could do nothing because we were out of their grasps forever. The lake itself was nothing special; special only in that it was water and water somehow is always special, as long as it was mostly water, compositionally. This lake was mostly water with some sewage but we could ignore the sewage with our innate ability to ignore dirt; this ability was essential for survival.

At the lake we met—old friends now fancy and adultish, with great futures and responsibilities. Everyone spoke of this college and those exams and factories and businesses, but I had nothing to say and was silent. A few others were silent too, not because they had nothing and were losers like me but because they were modest and spoke only when spoken to and did not have that desire to hijack, however gently, a conversation.

Finally, I would make an excuse and leave earlier than everyone else because the pressure to say something became overwhelming and it was tempting to lie. And they would say, 'Ib, stay for a bit, man. Charu got some beer.' But I couldn't stay; not because of them, but because of me. There was something inside me that didn't like other people.

59

* * *

One day Ajju was important and said officially, 'Ib, what about college? That St Peter's is very good.'

'For what, Ajju?' I asked. I had no idea what to do.

'Listen now,' he said, 'it's about time you begin to think about what you want to do. How long has it been since school? Three months. Rukku, why isn't he writing exams?'

My mother muttered something weakly from behind the bead curtain in the kitchen.

'Bloody hell! Is there no one in this house who cares what this boy does? Your father obviously can't, at least the mother.'

He stood up heavily. 'I'm going to speak to the principal,' he said. 'By next week, I want you to decide your subjects.' With those future-killing words, he walked out.

But what about my dreams? What was the record for deciding one's dreams? One month? One year? But I had no dreams and so had to start from scratch.

The next few days, irritated and angry, I roamed about, not with my usual laziness but with a great angry purpose as if the sheer force with which I hit the air would forge new paths in my future and close the gaps in my past. But the walking just annoyed me further. This was when I went first into a pub which I had seen many times before. In school I had heard it was the cool place to be, where everyone went to have a good time, and I guessed, to drown out the bad times. And what was it that attracted me to that smoky place? The smoke, the drink; a place in which the races were all put on hold and everyone took part with pleasure in their mutual destruction. And it was beautiful—the hatred of health, the malevolence towards restraint, the letting-go as if in this space everything was permitted and nothing mattered. In this place god was truly dead and another god was in place, the god of pleasure.

In truth there was a race and that was to get in each other's pants, but luckily everyone was so junked that nobody cared too much even if they were rejected and humiliated.

That was the thing about drinking, I found—that the alcohol drowns out discretion and facts until you're just a clown in a smart pair of pants amusing the pretty girls and embarrassing yourself. It was a relief from daily life.

Appoos meanwhile was getting worse. One morning I stood my ground and said to mother, 'We have to get him help. Yesterday he called me a traitor, accused me of conspiring with the walls to keep him trapped.' She didn't look up from the pan and was quiet. Then she said, 'I don't think we can afford it.'

'What about Ajju?' I asked.

'You want to tell him that's fine, but don't blame me then if everyone looks at us strangely.'

'It's not about us, it's about Appoos. I can't bear to look at his eyes like that any more,' I said. She turned around, surprised. 'You've grown, Ib, I think you can make this decision yourself. I'm weak, I know I'm weak,' her voice broke and she sobbed. 'If only things had turned out differently with him. We could have travelled.'

'I know, Ma, I know. Don't cry like that. We'll get him better.'

I left the kitchen, past the rosewood desk by the window, and it seemed to be watching in hard silence, and I felt like everything was watching, such was the seriousness of the moment. Appoos was by the window in his room, staring out. Sometimes he cried, sometimes he laughed. Today he was just sitting there, light on his crumbly face, with distant eyes and absent mind. I walked up behind him and placed my hand on his shoulder. He didn't move. 'Appoos, you

61

want some juice?' 'Get me juice, get me juice,' he said. 'I told you to get me juice.'

Visiting my grandfather wasn't the most exciting or pleasant experience a human can have. First, you had to make sure you had your speech ready. He was a very formal man, and believed in presentation and appearance, and first impressions. But his house was strangely bare. Perhaps Ajju was one of those people who pretended to be living a life much more luxurious than the reality of his surroundings, or perhaps he cared less for things than we thought. Past the thin metal gate and the low white wall was a tidy garden, thin and clipped, not a shrub more than a foot high, green and maroon leafed plants and aloe vera horns, a strip of yellow and red flowers, and towards the house a line of rose plants that never flowered. The house itself was a large white structure, with simple and obvious angles, without any modern architectural trickery, or any traditional bling, just white *chunna*, red tiles and brown windows, black bars. I knocked on the door, brown and plain, yet imposing as if it knew on whose orders it stood straight-backed, a wooden Janus, watching the inside as well as the outside, watching, watching and protecting. Ajju opened the door and Silly was out in a flash, Silly the excited, old Beagle, the only creature with whom Ajju spoke gently. I shook Ajju's hand and he let me in. Silly was in in a flash, bouncing on his hind legs, reaching for my face. I stroked his head and he calmed down, licking my hand. I said, 'Ajju, Silly's grown so old!' He smiled tenderly. 'Yes, she's an old dog, but has the energy of a younger dog,' he said and I wasn't sure if he was talking about the dog. 'So what do you want?' he asked. He was always getting to the point of things. We sat down.

'Ajju, Appoos is very sick. We need to take him to a doctor,' I said, trying to keep my voice objective and planned, but inside I shook like a flag in a storm, cold and alone against black clouds.

He was silent for a minute. Then when the silence was over he said, 'I don't know what you want from me. I'll give you the money, but it's stupidity, I tell you, this ridiculous thing of going to a doctor to get your mind right. All he needs is some discipline and some calm. Tell your mother to leave him alone for a few days at the ashram. I have been told many times how the Swamy has cured people of the so-called mental illness. Send Kamran to a doctor, any doctor you want, and let him talk to anyone, and if that doesn't help him, send him to the ashram.'

I nodded and couldn't speak. My throat felt frozen, as if cemented with the anger of this moment, of the ignorance of the powerful, at the same time with the relief from the years of suffering. I stood, and Ajju patted me on the back. 'I'm glad you came, Ib. It's nice to see you in my house. Here I feel calmer.' I crouched and played with Silly for a minute, then got up to leave. As I shut the door behind me, I turned and saw my grandfather leaning against the wall and looking down at the unfriendly floor.

On my way home, it was getting dark and the wind began to do its dance. I felt a great burden lifted from the back of my neck and I walked freer. I was angry still with

Ajju's ignorance and old-fashioned ideas, yet he wasn't a cruel man, I knew, because he didn't force his ignorance upon us. When I stopped at a cigarette shop, the man looked at me strangely, as if he knew I had overcome a great obstacle, defeated a large enemy of happiness and progress, but he was probably just looking at my hair, which looked like a home for a small animal. He looked puzzled too at my dirty jeans and my ironed shirt. Who is this strange looking man in my neighbourhood, he must have thought. I reached home late, and mother was asleep. I could hear Appoos's snores, and silence. I sat down, tired and happy. Should I write mother a note to tell her the good news? I couldn't decide, wondering if it would be a waste of good news. She wasn't good at taking good news, and usually received it with the same face as bad news. Finally, I decided that I should. There was always a notepad by the phone. I picked it up and scribbled on it. I wrote, 'All done. Ajju says OK.' Then I snuck up the stairs, careful to avoid the wind chimes at the top, and collapsed on my bed. For the first time in my life, it felt like I had achieved something worth collapsing for. The next morning, it was all the same, and I felt a brief moment of anger at Amma for being the way she was. She was making dosas and Appoos sat at the window, watching something outside, chuckling to himself. The note lay there by the phone but I could see that it had been handled. I decided not to say anything about the whole matter but Appoos turned suddenly to me and said, 'Your mother is sad, Ib. Ask your mother why she's sad.' Mother was standing in

64

the kitchen pouring out coffee into small steel glasses. 'What happened?' I asked. She didn't say anything. 'Did you read the note?'

She nodded and finally a sob broke through her defence. 'Thank you, Ib,' she said. I smiled and said nothing. Appoos banged on the chair. 'Breakfast,' he shouted. 'Ohhh breakfast.'

* * *

If Appoos was being shifted to a hospital, which the doctor advised us to do, would I need to stay at home, I asked mother. At first she didn't say anything, which was normal, then she changed her mind and insisted that I leave. 'You need to live your life,' she said, folding clothes into a small, black suitcase. 'Don't waste your youth on your mother.' I tried to argue but she continued, 'Don't pity me, please. This is what I want. For years now, I've only been cooking and cleaning for Appoos. Now that he's gone, I want to read books and watch TV. Have you seen all the channels these days? They say I can watch wildlife channels all day.' 'And I'll visit him, of course,' she added hastily, looking embarrassed. 'Once a week at least.' Finally, her packing was done. She was to stay with Appoos for a few days to settle him in, then she would come back and begin her life. Already I could see a kind of freeness in her, like when a dog is released from his leash, but doesn't know it for a few minutes, yet his movements become more and more till he suddenly realizes and bounds away happily. And maybe she would bound away happily, but I couldn't see it. Mother, unlike a dog, was not a happy thing. It had

65

been too long since she had felt the sensation of an open wind in her hair, or had heard the rustle of dry leaves by a summer breeze. The house had become a crucible of its own sounds and smells and her brain was cooked by this lethal hyper-local mixture.

There was a shop by the bridge that sold cable TV, a miraculous technology that brought channels from America and Europe right into our living rooms. Or that's what they said at least. It was expensive but if I was to leave home, I had to leave something appropriate behind. There was money left over from the registration process at the hospital that everyone had forgotten about. I paid in full and the smooth-faced, oily-haired man, with his background of hanging objects, pencils, paper, tape and other motley items, smiled the kind of smile that come from somewhere bad, and said, 'Two days, guarantee.'

A week later, a grumpy, pot-bellied creature appeared at our doorstep with a reluctant expression and half-tucked brown shirt. He grunted and carried a carton full of wires and a wrench up the stairs. When he finished attaching the cables on the roof and finally plugged it into our TV, there was a gasp from Amma who was standing quietly behind, as channel after channel flickered on and on, on the old box. The technician clicked the remote and was utterly bored, looking up at the peeling ceiling. He left as unhurried and upset and grumpy as he came. Amma was transfixed and excited. She even dragged Appoos into the room like a little child showing her father a butterfly.

A few cold months passed with Appoos in the hospital. He was blind now (the medication had some unfortunate and unforeseen side-effects), and they said (those white coats still white at the end of the day) that he was prime material to be a torturer to his caregiver. Amma heard this and her lips quivered as if to say, 'What? It's been a while since someone told me something I already know. It's been like that for years. What do you know? What do you care?' all in one little quiver. (I am a watcher, did I mention, and do not react to the screams of my little subjects.) When we went to the hospital to see Appoos, the Malayali nurse who was assigned to him gave us the wrong ward and that took us through the entire length of the hospital that delayed death. She was gone later and Amma couldn't glare at her (which was the most any of us would have done), and when we did find Appoos, Vikram Uncle was there, on his phone. He looked angry and annoyed and left without saying a word. The room looked out over a middle-garden, surrounded on all sides by little rooms with small square windows in the white walls. The sheets were white, too, the steel was cold and some flowers were never dead—they were plastic. Someone had scribbled: 'Who watches the watchers?' by the toilet door, a question that I was afraid would never be answered. At least life had a simple answer, made clear by the building I stood in; and if death wasn't a direct answer to life, perhaps it was more of a footnote, as one can see in serious papers about meaning and reality.

When everyone left, Appoos and I were left behind watching the silent television with the voiceless anchor shouting, as a thousand terrible tragedies flickered on screen behind her. Appoos drank juice through a straw; and when he finished the last few drops (he would know by the slurp) he kept the straw. There was a pile now: forty-one straws, one every day. And he kept them by the side table, and would let his hand drop every now and again, and speak while his fingers did the counting. 'Oh, Ibn Batuta,' he would say as I entered. 'See the great explorer comes to seek treasure.' To seek treasure in the house of death wasn't the best kind of exploring, I would reply, but my voice already beaten down by the misery all around, would drown in the laughter of Appoos and his bald roommate.

He was finally sane: The doctors had done their work. But the world every day was dark and noisy. Faceless nurses changed the sheets; shapeless forms pushed his bed; strange voices addressed him like they knew him. By the end of the day he was restless, counting the straws too quickly, not really counting, but just letting them pass through his fingers and holding them briefly.

'I used to see some great colours,' he said one day, turning his face towards where he thought I sat, but I had moved away a long time ago, sitting by the window and watching dust and traffic. 'But now I know I was lost then.' And then suddenly sensing something he added, 'Ib, are you there? Are you leaving now?'

'No, Appoos, I'm here.' But I wasn't. I was far away. I was cheating on my father.

I took to walking through the smell-less corridors, and watched the general suffering, like the wandering Jew for

68

whom war was temporary; and knew the weather in terms of climate; and for whom change was so vast that he knew nothing at all. I felt like this, completely fucked by this overdose of misery, till there was nothing I knew. Facts were useless to me; and so was hope; and the only thing that mattered was that the sheets were being changed every day—this at least seemed something practical and useful, and the dust that collected on the grey crucifixes that hung on the wall above every bed suggested that the nurses felt that way too, but very, very deep inside.

FIVE

To take control of my dreams and to further his ordinary ideas, Ajju made an appointment at St Peter's College for the following week. Amma wasn't allowed to come, even though she was alone at home and had no responsibilities and was done cleaning the cupboards. But she couldn't press against her father's pushiness, and this was the state of her entire life, of not pushing against pushing, and thus was constantly jostled into sad and lonely situations. As we left she said to me, pulling me aside as Ajju became busy with which route was best, 'Babu, feel the college with your heart. Don't just listen to others.' I knew what she meant by other and knew she referred only to the one other who was checking the car's tyres unnecessarily.

When we reached—we took a route that was long and busy—Ajju was in a terrible mood because of his miscalculation. 'Goddamn police,' he said, as the car shuddered to a halt in the college parking lot, 'every day they change something, one-way one day, the next it's two-way. I'm going to speak to the commissioner.'

The route was in fact exactly the same as it had been. Put it down to my fear and insecurity, and my lack of trust in anything driven by a human brain, but I was always acutely aware of navigation and our whereabouts, since the time I had eyes to see and a neck long enough to watch, and I knew for a fact, verified by experience, that this specific route had never changed.

In the admission office, his face had loosened slightly, massaged by the therapeutic effect of moving-out-of-the-way and hush-making respect, but still he had to appear strict and commanding, which overall resulted in some of the ugliest and nastiest looking smiles to ever grace a human face, take history and all. It turned out, as I was made aware of only later, that he was on the board, which explained his choice, and explained my lack of choice, as if he was saying secretly but just loud enough for me to hear that I wasn't good enough to get into colleges in which we didn't have levers of influence embedded deep into its machinery. And he was probably right too.

At the VC's office there was no waiting and the people who were waiting didn't even blink when we walked right past them into the room, so deep were they in the rigged game of arbitrary delays.

I already hated the VC when I spotted him behind his much-too-big desk. He had a rotten face that was up to no good even at that very moment, I remember thinking, just below the desk, where we could not see. And just like all rotten men, there was no neutrality of tone and he spoke very differently to different people; one way to power, one way to the slave, one way to those who were neither.

To Ajju, of course, he crooned almost, bending forward at the hip, pulling out chairs and asking for coffee (his tone changing mid-sentence as he turned to the peon, who waited in the corner, and ordered coffee).

'Sir, this is your grandson, sir? Ib, is it? Very good, sir.' He barely looked at me, just once confirming my presence with his eyes, and then directed everything exclusively at my grandfather. It was as if my going to college there was just a byproduct of other larger and more important agendas which I would never understand.

All the papers were signed (by Ajju), and there was a lot of thanking and platitudes. When it was time to leave I said thank you to the VC and he smiled and said that it was no problem at all, but behind the smile there was a sneer of resentment.

In the car Ajju told me that he was old friends with the VC, Mr Ramesh. 'You know who his father is? He started the college. He was a big man, very nice man. His son also, very good fellow. Don't you think so, Ib?' I grunted and stared out the window. That explained how that nasty rodent could be the vice chancellor of a big college. And it explained at once a lot about everything, this net of connections that held the rich and dirty few above the toughness and sewage of the ground far below.

'Ajju, how did you get on the board?' I asked.

'After retirement, you know I was a General. I was invited by Ramesh's father,' he said.

'But why you, Ajju?'

'See, I was highly decorated. He wanted someone with principles, someone who could manage other people. Because people, you see, are lazy and stupid mostly. Only a few are able to handle things. You'll understand one day, Ib, how these things work. How people work together.'

This is not working together, I thought, and was sure there was something else behind it, something dark.

'We'll drop in at the temple, Ib. We should give thanks to god,' he said shortly. 'The problem is when things are going good, nobody thanks god, but when things are bad, everyone is on their knees and crying.'

I laughed because he was right and that pleased him deeply and he immediately became jolly and began to hum a song from an old movie. Once in a while he honked with the tune.

73

Once at the temple he grew serious again, as if joy and enjoyment were emotions one wasn't supposed to display in front of god, lest they think the source of the mirth was immoral and cheap. Inside, it was cool and quiet and smelt of coconut oil and camphor.

Facing the idol (of whom I did not know), he sank to his knees and bowed his head to the floor. This was the thing to do, I guessed, and did the same, but curiously nothing seemed to happen anywhere, either outside or inside, and I grew confused, sitting there on my haunches, next to my old Ajju. And through the corner of my eye I tried to see what I was doing, if the technique was wrong, or perhaps my spot unholy, but in the temple, all the space was holy surely.

'Close your eyes,' Ajju said suddenly. Ah, so this was the secret. Slowly and with great reverence I shut out the world and sat still. Still nothing! All I could hear was his soft mumbling and some temple bells in the distance— no holy voices, no supernatural whispers. Something was missing.

Suddenly it struck me—how would god answer if you don't first ask? He has many things to do and can't always keep all channels open.

'Please, god,' I began, 'let my parents live forever. Please make college easy.'

There was no answer.

Outside the inner sanctum, god's VIP lounge, Ajju stretched his legs and dropped a few notes in a vessel that was placed outside. The priest pretended not to notice the exact amount.

In the car again, I asked Ajju why god didn't talk back and Ajju said, 'god only listens. He never answers. You must have faith.' This to me seemed unnecessarily complicated and could create a lot of confusion.

But wait! In this point in the future I mix up the dim past. This visit to the temple did happen but it was much earlier and probably not even with Ajju, though I don't remember. By the time I went to meet the VC with Ajju, all my illusions about talking idols had vanished and I remember, yes, I remember now, that I had sat silently by my grandfather on that day, and wished with all my heart that I could go away and escape his wrinkly grasp.

* * *

In March the trees came alive, baby pink, yellow, by the side of the roads, and in quiet neighbourhoods. From a roof I could see the city, bursts of pink and yellow, in seas of green, then suddenly, sharp, concrete and ugly, bluish glass. The city didn't need to look at itself in the mirrors of these modern buildings because the city had had enough of itself, and so had the people. But there was a joyous pleasure in walking along the rows of trees boiling with baby pink and white flowers; under my feet the fallen flowers, and for once I could ignore the office on the other side of the road from which thousands came and went, bagged and tagged. Soon the flowers would disappear and the land would turn brown and a great heat would come about, the giant heat of the sun, beating down on those who didn't sit in air-conditioned offices. In summer, there was only one god—air-conditioning. In winter, many gods because we didn't really have a winter.

75

On the last day of the second year of college, I quit and stayed home for a week. There was nothing for me there, and my mind felt beaten and faded every time I sat in a class. The teachers were just doing their job and my classmates had their beady eyes firmly on the future, so firmly that they didn't notice the rot around them. One evening, drunk and reckless, Major, a new friend, and I, made our way down a road. It was late March, and the flowers were dry carcasses on the pavement, little pink ballet frocks, and there was a warmth in the air, an omen of the heat to come. Major was pleased about something, skipping over the broken pavement at every opportunity and laughing to himself. When we reached the end of the road, we stopped and looked around, not sure where to go. 'Let's go up the station,' said Major, pointing vaguely towards the Metro, and grinning stupidly. I was reluctant; but after a few drinks, reluctant wasn't an emotion I took very seriously. So we climbed the barrier and hopped down the other side. It was quiet and dark. The last train was long gone, and a lonely security guard slept deeply in the corner, his large stomach rising and falling. Major whispered something and I followed him, trying to control my laughter. We climbed the stairs and reached the platform. 'Hey, don't go on the tracks,' I said. 'They're electrified.' 'Not at this time,' whispered Major. He stood at the edge of the platform looking down. 'Are you sure?' I asked. He wasn't. He turned to me and suddenly there was a look in his eyes, a look of fear. 'Major?' I said with warning in my tone. 'What are you doing?'

'Maybe we don't know,' he said, 'maybe sometimes we should take a chance and let fate decide.' I stepped quickly towards him and took him by his arm. 'OK, this way. Let's talk about that over a drink, not over electrified rails. You heard about that girl who died last week?' He looked relieved, as if I had saved him from himself but he tried to be casual. 'I was just kidding. You really think I would have . . .' And suddenly bang came the lights and we looked over our shoulders. The fat security guard running towards us, whistling desperately, his stomach reluctant to obey the commands of gravity and his cane swinging in his hand. By the time he reached us he was so tired that he could barely move and stood there, hands on knees, shouting something we couldn't understand. We laughed and laughed and he kept shouting. Then we heard a single word that shut us up. The word was 'police'.

I tried to reason with him as he jostled us down the stairs with his cane, but he grunted and poked me harder. Major was still laughing and egging me on to negotiate.

'Sir, never again. We are very sorry,' I pleaded. But he was determined.

'You rich kids come here thinking you can do anything,' he said. 'You need to be taught a lesson.'

'But I'm not rich.'

'Richer than me.'

'We can work that out,' said Major but the guard ignored him.

But it was too late and we had reached the bottom of the stairs and on the road we saw the cops on their Cheetah bike. They came towards us with a shared, kind of cruel, eager grin. 'Trespassing,' said the fat one.

'Illegal drinking,' said the other fat one.

'Who are you?' asked the fat one.

'What are you doing here?' asked the other fat one.

Major explained and they immediately agreed that it wouldn't be good for either us or them if Major was taken to jail. We gave them Rs 100 and they left, struggling with their bike and their stomachs, convinced of victory. We grinned at the guard who held out his hand. 'Tea, saar,' he said sadly. Major took out another note and said, 'Next time we'll bring our friends.' He placed the note in the guard's grimy palm and the guard nodded and smiled, having forgotten his earlier stridency. We left in a hurry.

'That was exciting,' Major said, lighting a King. He had forgotten all about the tracks. 'So you're the assistant commissioner's son?' I asked. 'No, I'm not,' he said happily. 'Or maybe sometimes.' The rest of the walk back we were quiet. I watched the black night and the orange lights, and the few silent people whom we passed. What were they doing, I wondered, on such a fine night, alone and silent? What had they learnt? I had learnt something, something scary about Major, from his eyes, and I couldn't sleep the whole night.

The next morning I staggered in late and the teacher said, 'How can you be so useless?' And that was that. I quit the next day, telling the VC that we were moving cities, some sort of family emergency. He waved a juicy hand at me and let me go.

A few days later, Amma came to me huffing with nervousness and fear. 'Ib, you better get a job,' she said. Immediately she began to fold clothes. She did this and she felt calm.

'What's the hurry?' I asked. She folded the last T-shirt and sat down at the edge of the bed.

'Ajju heard you quit college. He's coming here tomorrow.'

'Who told him? Nobody knew.'

'Probably the VC.'

I thought for a moment. 'Amma, just tell him I have a job in Bagram's office,' I said.

'But you don't, Ib.' She looked down sadly at the floor because she didn't like to lie, at the same time she saw that there might be a necessity to do so now. The conflict was clear on her worried face and she began to fold clothes again, the same ones she had already done, unfold, then fold, in some different way.

'I'll get one. He told me to come to him when I needed a job,' I said, trying to reassure her, but it wasn't working and she looked up at me.

'Why, Ib? Do you think he'll just give you a job? You don't have any skills or experience. This is not how the world works.'

I always tried to be gentle with Amma because she was a soft person and harsh words harmed her more than they harmed other people. And her intentions were good too mostly.

'Maybe he sees something in me, Ma,' I said.

She smiled sadly and it seemed like some long-forgotten light shone in her memories, of a long lost past when she looked at her son and saw hope and happiness. But quickly that light was gone and she got up from the bed.

'Anyway, I hope you know what you're going to say, babu,' she said and left, closing the door behind her.

79

I felt myself for the first time in a jam, the kind that adults always speak and write about, the kind of jam that sprouts books and movies, jams of the adult world. This was the bridge I had stumbled over when I quit college, the bridge from being a safe and harmless child to a dangerous and consequential adult, because college is where a black-and-white childhood ends and adulthood creeps in like a grey moss that clings to your insides for the rest of your life. And everything becomes grey for a time, then you begin to see the shades of grey, some light, some dark, and you learn your place in the world.

So I prepared a great and elaborate lie about a job. I knew Ajju and Mr Bagram didn't get along very well, because Ajju had called him a 'crooked little black man', but I also knew that because Ajju had said such a cruel thing against him he was actually a good man. So in this swamp of dislike between these two large men, I could build my castle of lies, and it would remain upright at least till I actually built a life for myself, and then it wouldn't matter any more what Ajju said and the things he shouted.

Ajju arrived early the next morning and sat at the table expecting breakfast, and Amma was having a tough time because he hadn't told her he was coming this early. 'There's not much food,' she said, hurrying round the kitchen. 'Fine, Ib, go get some dosas,' he commanded, then added, 'Why don't you ask for money if you need it?' Amma opened her mouth to argue but thought better of it. There was no better way of ruining everyone's day than arguing with Ajju.

His bald head glistened in the watery morning light, and for an instant I felt the great burden that Amma had carried and the misery he had brought her and in that instant I suddenly thought, 'What if I just plunged a knife into his dirty bald head?' but thought better of it because Amma was there and she would be traumatized by the blood. I went out quickly before my mouth got the better of my mind, and was barely aware of the short cycle ride to the dosa shop; the steam that rose from behind the counter, five or six working people sitting alone staring ahead blankly as they hurried through another breakfast, in such a hurry, and going about the first food of the day with such little pleasure that they hadn't even removed their backpacks from their rounded and featureless backs. I was back soon, and Ajju had moved to the sofa with a cup of coffee and the newspaper, and Amma sat behind on the table peeling garlics and looking utterly miserable. It seemed he had already begun the process of being angry. When I entered, Amma looked up but Ajju's gaze didn't move from his paper. I held up the dosas and Amma nodded sadly. 'He ate,' she said and Ajju smiled. I sat down and he finished reading the paper. Then he folded it and placed it carefully on the table.

'What do you think you're doing?' he asked after a brief silence.

'What, Ajju? I'm going to get a job and . . .'

'You fool. How dare you? I was the one who got you into that college. You think you can just run away when you want? I'm on the board. What are they going to think?

You know what Aruna said the other day? She said the board has to be more careful with recommendations. Do you know what she meant?' Spit flew from his large mouth and his face shuddered. Amma's head was even lower now and the pace at which she peeled the garlic had grown rapidly.

'Ajju, will you listen . . .'

'Shut up,' he said, 'shut up and you listen. This is the problem with you. You think you know everything.'

'No, I don't know everything but I do know this is not good for me.' My voice was raised too and this seemed to surprise Amma who had stopped peeling and sat staring at us.

'Again you're talking as though you know everything,' he said, getting up from the sofa. 'How do you know it's not doing good? The benefits of college are felt years later, not next day or next week. You young people these days, you think you can do your own damn thing, you think this world is some garden or palace where you'll be welcomed and made comfortable? Nothing works like that.'

I felt like fighting and screaming. I felt like telling him that inside me there was something that needed to move about, to explore, to find things for myself, to look at things from high up and down below, to feel the misery of insecurity, the misery of poverty, the agony of unemployment, to feel at once, everything and nothing, high and low, Left and Right, the atom and the universe, the soul of a single child, and the collective sadness of humanity, all at once, and by myself, to be alone in darkness so one day I could climb out into a better light. And textbooks and engineering degrees weren't going to get me any of these things. But I didn't fight and was quiet as the torrents of his anger at being humiliated fell over me like a large and stinging wave. Because I was sure, he didn't care about me or my future, rather the whispers among teachers and board members when they saw him in the hallways, whispers of maybe he wasn't such a great man after all, because his grandson was a college dropout and these things run in the blood.

Finally he was finished and he wiped his face with a handkerchief that he always carried and put away in the back pocket of his pants. Then he tried being gentle and said, 'Ib, you are young, you must learn the consequences of your actions. Everything you do now, will matter later. This is how you must live. Trust me, you have to go to college.'

He sat down again, and he looked tired. I had taken a lot from him that evening and I felt sorry for that old bald man. I apologized for raising my voice and he said, 'No, Ib, don't apologize. I started shouting.' And then, after a minute, he looked at me again and said, 'So will you join again? I can speak to them.'

I shook my head and his face once again grew hard and sharp.

'I'm warning you,' he said, 'I'm warning you, don't ruin your future, boy.' With that he stood up forcefully and walked out of the room. That gentleness was also a tactic to get his way, but he had returned to his default

83

anger. His tone carried that and it was evident that he was trying his best to save his careful, efficient, systematic image. If it wasn't for this image, he would have begged, but appearances have to be kept up in many places at once, and in that way life becomes a web of appearances.

And he went out trying his best to appear unaffected.

* * *

I couldn't face Ajju any more and so avoided him all that I could. But sometimes things couldn't be helped and I would meet him at home, and we tried not to look at each other. Mother couldn't have been less bothered and was probably quite relieved that she didn't have to do any more peacekeeping between us. Once we almost collided in the corridor and neither acknowledged the other. He made a huff, I was silent and we passed, but suddenly I remembered the stories he used to tell me when I was a child, and I felt sad. 'Ajju,' I called after him, but he had disappeared into the house and I was on my way out.

Later, mother told me that he had stopped when I called out, but only for a second. Then he was gruff the rest of the day, and worse than usual. Thus a meeting was avoided for the good of everyone and not just the two parties involved. And it was also good for me because I didn't have to get tangled, even verbally, with Ajju's new hobby, spirituality, which he insisted to Amma was completely different from religion, yet I didn't see any difference in the way he spoke about it. Only the word 'god' was never mentioned, but other euphemisms and more sophisticated, polished words, like gems, words like 'some supreme energy', a 'supreme force', 'higher consciousness', things that did the work of that old and unfashionable word god were. There was a noticeable change in him after he took up this new pastime. He was less direct, more peaceful, but not correctly peaceful like the gurgle of a mountain stream, but peaceful like the silence in the corridor of a prison when a man is on death row and making his last walk to the galleys, a threatening peace, the kind of peace that says, 'Soon you will suffer and die.' He did things indirectly now, said things with deflection and falseness, as if we weren't worth his anger any more, and since we were godless and materialistic idiots, the only good that could be done for us, was prayer and silence. When he wanted things, he would put it as if he didn't really want them for his personal satisfaction, rather he wanted them for the general good of humanity as a whole, as though everyone would benefit if he was given a fried egg for lunch. Everyone knows the truest sacrifice is the one that is not talked about. But when he was inconvenienced in any way, he would make it out to be great sacrifice, never once saying either that he had sacrificed something great, or that he was upset by the sacrifice, but saying too many times exactly the opposite, saying, 'It's OK. The food was less tasty, but it's OK, I don't care about taste anyway, I eat for nutrition. A man must be simple and not have desires.' This was coming from a man who told everyone every chance he got how the commissioner of police came to see him in 1992.

Sprouting from this new hobby was a greater interest in temples and holy men. 'They are among us to show us the

Truth,' he would say about filthy and half-naked crazy old coots who begged at traffic signals and grinned horribly at children, hair matted with dirt, teeth orange with tobacco and shit.

There was a temple on a hill nearby. Ajju began to go there often and came back with stories of a sadhu who lived there. 'That man is enlightened,' he said. 'I will build him a shrine.' He began to make arrangements; called contractors, bought bricks, then came back one evening, face red with anger. 'That crazy old bastard,' he shouted, 'he told me to get lost. He's just a crazy old man.' But the next week there was another sadhu who sat in some other temple for whom Ajju wanted to build a shrine. 'He is a true saint,' he said at dinner, 'a fully realized man.' So work began on this updated shrine (the sadhu was only too happy to oblige), and Ajju spoke loudly of how the sadhu had blessed him and promised him a happy afterlife.

It was the fear of death that had got into his flawless bald head. Once an efficient and reasonable commander, Ajju had lost the confidence that reasonable men have, and was now afraid of everything. But still he pretended to be in control. It was pathetic to watch and involved a lot of lying and evasion.

To avoid Ajju, his curly temper, his heavy presence, it was no longer a sane or dutiful thing to stay at home because his visits grew more frequent, probably to scare me. And perhaps he wanted me out. Who knew? Even though I was his only grandson. And so I obliged and spoke to Amma in the evening and told her I wanted to go. 'Not too far, babu?'

'No, Ma,' I said.

'But who will you stay with?'

'Major and me are sharing an apartment. It's his uncle's, so no rent.'

She stirred a pot slowly, looking into it as if our fortunes were indicated in the cut of the curry, the spice or the thickness, the way it flowed.

'Ma, I'll visit so often you won't even know,' I said cheerfully.

Smiling sadly, she dipped a spoon into the pot. 'Taste it, Ib, maybe it's the last time.' I protested loudly and she said she was joking and pushed the spoon in my mouth. The curry was tasteless and cold but I told her it was the best she had ever made.

'Say bye to Appoos,' she said. It had been a month since he came back from the hospital and almost back to his old self—nuts, but with 20/20 vision.

'Should I tell him? Or should I say I'm going out?'

She looked sternly at me and said, 'Ib, he's crazy, not stupid. What if tomorrow he asks? Tell him the truth but tell him you'll come back often and watch TV.'

I hugged her, halfly, side-form, because she was back to cooking, and left the kitchen.

Appoos was watching TV, a Discovery Channel show on volcanoes. 'Ib, you're back,' he shouted. I smiled and sat next to him. We watched the show in silence. When it was over he said, 'These people are brave, they go near the volcano, what if it explodes, baba?' I told him they are willing to take the risk. 'What about their families?' he asked with great concern in his face, 'do they not have families?'

'I'm sure they do, Appoos,' I said.

'Then how can they leave like that? What do they tell their wives, their sons? I'm going to a volcano and I may never come back?'

He began to sob and I rubbed his back. 'Appoos, they know when the volcano is going to erupt so they go only when it's peaceful.'

He stopped sobbing and thought. 'Yes, they know when the volcano is angry,' he said confidently. Then he was silent and his eyes became blank and he slipped in and out of some internal world. I looked into that grizzly grey face and suddenly felt great pain. It was as if staring too long into the abyss that he was in would mean the abyss for me, a certain and black path into the depths of madness. And to think the abyss was in the midst of my father, like a black hole in the middle of our galaxy, was a pain so great that I got up with a start and looked away. He didn't stir. I waited for a few seconds and decided I didn't want to tell him. Let Amma deal with him, I thought, and slipped out quickly.

* * *

The apartment was in an old building, greyed and greened by age, hands, smoke, moss, graffiti in the elevators, scratched paint. The corridors and staircases were unlit and echoing and carried the collective muffled sounds of every apartment in the block. Crackling radios, murmuring televisions, crying babies, whistling cookers, shifting furniture, shouting men, shrill women, loud boys, hassled girls; and the scents—an unbalanced mix of sambar, fish, steaming rice and other unrecognizable things. Wilting plants were placed outside every door, and bored women in nighties watched from their barred kitchen windows as you crossed the empty corridors. Ours was on the third floor, bare as a desert, but cooled by lucky cross ventilation. Featureless, furniture-free, we sat and slept on thin grey cotton mattresses that were lumpier than a mud road, so one had to manoeuvre and sleep carefully. But quickly it became home, with the freedom that homes are meant to have, not with comfort and convenience, because they can never replace the freedom of having no oppressive and suffocating presence.

I was mostly alone because Major had work and things to do and I had nothing. If I wanted to, I could have had something to do, but the new-found looseness of freedom kept me relaxed and calm. Soon I discovered there was no one to stop me from drinking beer or smoking all day if I wanted to, yet I didn't feel the need to drink a lot even though I could and in this I surprised myself. Major, returning from work, would begin drinking the moment he dropped his bag by the door. But I had no work, and nothing to hate, and so took it easy, lounged about and relaxed. Major would say, every evening, 'Have a drink, Ib.' We would drink together, sure, but he was quicker and was out before I was through my third. And every night I had to move his large and semi-solid form to his mattress. One night he suddenly opened his eyes and looked straight at me and he said, 'That girl, Ib, Annie, get her, Ib. You'll be good together.'

Later he told me Annie was a friend of his who was in college with us. I said, 'I have no idea who you're talking about.'

'Dark, dark eyes, quiet.'

I shrugged and he became hassled and tried to describe her again and again.

'OK, fine, I'll bring her one day, OK?' he said finally.

I said OK because there was nothing disagreeable about the idea, although the thought of putting effort into canoodling with the other sex just seemed an awful lot of trouble.

But I began to look forward to a visit from this dark Annie but it was constantly postponed by Major and his busyness, hurrying away. And every time it was delayed, my imagination filled in a little more, till finally the day she came, my mental picture of her was of some Amazonian goddess, a comic book superhero woman, with perfect, firm, powerful legs, smooth, perfect form, deep and piercing eyes, a flowing river of hair, holding a spear and floating above the ground from pure greatness. When I saw her, I was disappointed for a few minutes and then my brain adjusted. She said hi and we sat down. But it was soon clear that she had no interest in me and was more into what I was not doing, rather than doing. She thought I was wasting my time. I should be contributing to society, she said. The word society, which I found to be quite an expletive, turned me off and my mood dropped. She was a career woman, she said, and was being promoted, etc. Where did she work? In a publishing company. What did she do? Edit.

'I've thought about writing,' I said, and she gave me a sarcastic nod.

'Why don't you, then? Anyone can write.'

She sniggered and Major laughed and said, 'Hey, Annie, don't mock my friend. He has that kind of mind maybe, although I never thought about it.'

'Mind, no mind,' she said, 'makes no difference. Writing happens on paper, not in the head.'

'Ib, give it a shot,' said Major, 'I think you might do well.'

She was forcing her smile now. It seemed to upset her that Major thought I would make a good writer.

'You have to work at it,' she said again, 'it doesn't just form in your head.'

I was silent, and when she left, I thought about it. Would I make a good writer? The idea made me laugh. I was a shallow, lazy, cowardly little shit. How could I be a good writer? That was the last of that.

This meant that my relationship with Annie (whose name was Annamma) improved. We no longer had that bone to fight over—who was the better writer—and I found we got along well. She was trying to write a novel, she said, but her bread and butter was editing. 'How does it feel to edit other people's work when you want people to edit your work?' I asked her one evening at the old Watson's bar on the corner of our street.

She blinked her large dark eyes and looked into her drink.

'It sucks, Ib,' she said, 'but what can I do? If I quit work, I'll be broke and miserable. How do you survive without work?

'I manage,' I told her. 'The trick is to lower your standard of living.'

'That's even tougher than writing a novel,' she replied, looking around at the rich young people wasting away their evenings in booze and cigarettes.

By the end of every one of our evening meets, we were both drunk and some games were played, the kind that two young single people play when they're drunk enough to flirt, yet not drunk enough to abandon all reason and tear each other's clothes off. And though there was nothing more I wanted to do—when she got close, I could smell the scent of her skin and feel the weight of her body, her face waiting to be held, her mouth close enough to see the moisture in the middle like—there was just enough brain in me to foresee the complications, Major, Annie, her other friends. I didn't even know if she had a boyfriend. That topic had never come up. And so we usually hugged and she clung on a little longer than was normal, I in my awkwardness, a little less than was appropriate, and as she drew away, she left the scent of her hair around my head like an ether of some deadly concoction that almost made me pass out.

But when Major was around, there was a sharpness to our interaction, all tightened up and cleaned, almost as if if we let go a little, we would collapse on to each other and then Major would be privy to the dirt in our minds, the filth in our dreams. Of course I assumed that this is what she felt, and as far as I know, it was accurate.

Before long, we were better friends than to be jealous and she began to encourage me to write, based upon the content of our conversations. She said I had something in me—a glint of quartz (not gold; gold was too precious) in the river mud—that made her sometimes sit up at night and think that I would be a better writer than she. This was quite a confession, she said, for anyone who harbours even the slightest creative urge; to admit that somebody else, especially someone close, was probably a better writer than they were.

'It pains me,' she said, 'but I think I'm a better editor than a writer, a better changer than a creator.' 93

This kind of disarming honesty was typical of her of late. It was a side she showed only to those she was close to, and it immediately thickened our relationship, to intimate levels and casual levels.

Obviously, finding work wasn't going to be easy, I knew, but I never considered a job to be so important, the pivot of an entire life. That seemed staid and unexciting, the sort of thing that only studious people did. I felt a need to explore, to move about freely in more than one building. The first few weeks I wandered about with no aim and no worry, but soon this became unexciting. I needed to find work, but the kind of work that didn't keep me pinned to one place. One day as we sat drinking, Major said, 'How about doing many jobs? Odd jobs, perhaps. You don't want money, so you can do that, no problem.' He was right.

* * *

They say if and when life throws you lemons, you must make lemonade, but what if you don't know how to make lemonade? Then you go about learning the technique. And to learn the technique by yourself is almost impossible, unless you are of the genius type, a rare type. I was no genius and needed help catching these lemons, cutting and squeezing them: How much sugar, how much salt and how much water? These are things that have to be learnt and discovered. Said Major, 'The more sour they are, the more difficult to make, yet the more you learn.' And a few weeks later, a big fat lemon came hurtling my way in the shape and form of an illness to my poor, dear mother. She was coughing blood and could barely speak. We took her to the hospital, and the doctors were concerned. One said, 'We have to do thorough check-ups.' Another just shook his head. The nurses were rude and laughed amongst themselves. Mother didn't object to any of it, or make one expression of pain. She felt, I think, that the tolerance of pain is the greatest good. But how were the doctors to know what she felt? With great reluctance she told them of a pain in her chest. Then it took only a few hours, and the younger doctor (the older one had left for the day) came in and patted my back and said everything is OK, it's just a lung infection, no cancer. When he said that word, we felt relief from a burden nobody had even spoken about but which hung around like a dark and threatening cloud on the horizon. But his words ushered in the sun like a great wind that parted those frightening clouds. But of course there was barely a reaction on her face as she lay there but she caught my eye and I could see her relief like the glint of gold in the darkness of a mine. Meanwhile, Ajju had arrived just in time for the good news and took command and spoke as if he had known all along. 'I had a feeling it was nothing serious,' he said knowledgeably to the young doctor who didn't seem very impressed and so a few minutes passed in which Ajju tried to appear more impressive and spoke about his contacts in the government. We still hadn't spoken since the incident and that icy silence remained as we made our way slowly down the stairs (Amma refused to take the lift and said it made her feel disabled). On our way back, Ajju wanted to stop at the temple, the one with the peepul tree. I wondered if we should perhaps take Amma back home first. 'She needs rest. Besides, Appoos will be awake by now, shouting for food,' I said tersely, not directly at him. 'Rest? That's why people get sick. What better sustenance than meeting with god?' Ajju scoffed. He ignored Appoos's plight.

At the temple, I held Amma's hand. Ajju went inside, first through the low door and the high step. We could hear the temple bells and the chants which nobody understood. Amma went in next, letting go of my hand at the last minute as she disappeared into the camphorous inner sanctum, and the peepul tree that rose above and over the low temple sighed with sadness. 'Here we go again,' it seemed to be saying, 'here come the desperate fools.'

It was empty that time of day. Amma and Ajju were nowhere in sight. I sat on the low cement platform that formed a seat around the tree and waited, and around me the sound of temple bells swirled.

I began to drift in and out of some strange dream of frogs and assassins. The world seemed unreal one minute and the next, it was rudely present, in my face, and the smell of camphor was in my head. Like an orange phantom, a sadhu had appeared suddenly and was standing right in front of me. I jumped up, mumbling apologies, but he didn't say a word and continued to stare at my face. 'What are you doing here?' he asked suddenly. I pointed towards the room where the idols were and mumbled. 'No, what are YOU doing here?' he said again.

I said, 'I had to come with them.' He didn't seem happy with my answer.

'Come tomorrow,' he said. 'Come tomorrow and we'll talk.' Then he turned and disappeared into his room. A moment later, his face appeared at the small window and his eyes were closed.

Mother had just come out from the room. 'Who was that?' she asked.

'No idea, Amma, just some nut.'

'Don't say things like that. He's a holy man.'

'I don't know about holy, but he's definitely crazy.'

'Shhh, Ajju is coming.'

'So why . . .'

'Ib!' she said with the kind of forcefulness that comes with fear.

Grandfather climbed over the high step and into the courtyard with that expression that religious people have after praying, as if they have done something so utterly humble and noble, an expression of self-righteous power and abject surrender at the same time. 'Ready?' he asked Amma. We climbed back in his Fiat and drove off just as the temple bells began again.

On our way back Ajju said angrily, 'A sadhu lives in that temple. He's a crazy fellow. Don't go to him.'

'Who's going to go, baba? Nobody is going,' Amma said and looked at me with a warning in her eyes.

'I'm just telling you, in case. He's mad. Not spiritual or anything, a fraud probably, will ask for money and then go and get drunk. You see one day we'll see him on the road completely tight.'

The rule that generally applied in my world of humans was that the people Ajju disliked and called mad were in reality excellent guys, marquee girls, and were capable and strong, and had independence and clarity. They were not sheep, not easy to herd or steer in the direction he liked. And so the sadhu who had appeared at the temple was probably quite a great man, and it was possible there was a lot to learn from him, despite his rudeness and abruptness. But I had learnt that abruptness in people was a good sign of entertainment or knowledge to come. I decided that I would go back to the temple as soon as possible, if only to spite Ajju.

97

When we reached, he was still grumbling. 'Crazy old fraud,' he was saying, 'one day he will be exposed. It will come in the paper. You see, I'm telling you now . . .'

* * *

It's not easy to tell which moment shaped your life, or steered it in any one way. Life forces are like a potter and life is clay and there is a gradual moulding that takes place, and the faster the wheel spins, the smoother you become. But suddenly, one force becomes too much and the clay is torn from the wheel and rips apart, flying everywhere, or is grotesquely deformed. So one must balance the influences that come from everywhere, all trying to mould you, all trying to spin the wheel faster and faster. One must be still, be centred, or the balance will tilt and you will be a crooked pot, taking in things crookedly, favouring one side over the other, and eventually things will accumulate on one side and begin to stink. If you befriend the potter, that's another matter, but there is no potter, only the pottery. These are some of my theories.

And so looking back, it would seem that choosing to go back to the sadhu was some form of cosmic pottery, and the mould was formed, shaped by unknown and old forces, the blood in our veins, the fog in our brains and the unstoppable physics of nature and the sun; the mould that the rest of my life would form in, germinate. How the final foliage would turn out was another matter, and obviously being small and stupid, I couldn't see beyond a few days.

And it was decided that I would go immediately, the next day, even if I didn't have time.

The next morning it was hot when I got out of the house, with that harsh heat that reminded me of factories and molten metal, not the wet heat of a coastal town, like a steam room. I reached the temple soaked in sweat, and was relieved to sit under the shade of the peepul tree. The sadhu came out of his room and sat on the cement and stone floor opposite, in a patch of shade. 'So you came?' he asked with an amused twinkle in his eye. I nodded and tried to speak, but he cut me short. 'I didn't ask you to speak,' he said, 'just sit and listen.'

So I sat and listened and this was what I heard. First, first because sounds come with an order, first was the sound of the peepul tree, a hushed rustle, like a thousand women in silk sarees doing a silent dance, then the wind, a low and distant howl like a lonely faraway wolf, then the birds, only one or two, alternating between loud chirping and a low short whistle. The sadhu pointed up towards the sky. Everything in the sky was silent—the clouds floated by and the sun, the most silent thing in the sky, beat down incessantly with its thousand bright white hammers on the vast land of my birth. The earth was brown and silent too, but within it, there was a world of worms and insects, small crawling rustling creatures who lived beneath our feet. This was the world below our world, the world that kept us up. And far away, a mosque cried and pigeons erupted into the air like loud smoke and dispersed, then the mosque was silent and another one then another one, a chain reaction of prayer and fools. Somewhere to my right and perhaps a few hundred yards away, a dog yelped and screamed and was silent. Suddenly the sadhu clapped, and the sound yanked me out of my soundscape. 'You see?' he said, 'the world around you. You are nothing but a part of it, a small and useless part. If you die, everything else will go on. You are nothing.' I was convinced by now that he was slightly unhinged, yet there was something refreshing in his craziness and lack of etiquette.

'Do you know what the world is?' he asked. I nodded.

'It is a vast arena of power and hatred, where the rich control everyone and everything with strings made of money and gold.'

'And yet here we are,' I said.

'Yes, here we are. That means nothing.'

'Doesn't it mean something? I am not here for money, neither are you.'

His face grew tense and his eyes narrowed.

'What do you know? You are a young man. Nothing you say or do now means anything. In a few years you too will be in that factory outside.'

'The factory needs to function,' I said, 'or how do you get your food, your bricks, your water?'

He didn't like what I was saying and stood up quickly. 'Do you think I want that?' he said loudly. 'But nobody leaves me alone. I don't want their food or their bricks. They came and built it around me.'

'You mean you were here first?' I asked.

'First, last, how does it matter? In the end, everything dies and is reborn.' He was a master of the pivot.

This was the first of my encounters with Mr Sadhu, and subsequently there would be many more. There was something in him, a strange mixture of wisdom and confusion, an accuracy of experience, yet no loyalty to the truth. It was clear he was an unchallenged type, and had lived his whole life without ever having been argued against, and this reflected in the way he argued. One morning he was naked and I didn't even bother asking him why, but he told me anyway, in that unhinged way that he spoke, that it was a matter of mother nature against society. 'What do you think, that humans can tell me what to wear and what not to wear?' he shouted. 'I do not take directions from fools.' And then in the next ten minutes, he was back in his orange robe, smoking a beedi, looking around suspiciously as if at any moment somebody would snatch it away. Why did I go there? Because it was a space where I didn't have to align with working people, and could just sit and stare at nothing, and nobody said anything. Outside, there were people in lines; here there were no lines, and very little order lingered. Mostly, when I visited, we sat on the stone and cement floor, and closed our eyes. Sometimes he cried, his shoulders shaking with the desperate escaping energy of his sobs, then in an instant, he was silent and still, and didn't even move his hands to wipe the tears that dripped down his beard and on to his sallow, thin-haired chest. Later, he wouldn't even acknowledge this and once said, 'What happens when I meditate is separate. If I did cry, it is but a side effect of something much higher.'

'Where do you go?' I asked.

'It is a different realm. Beyond thought and reason.'

'How is that possible? Are you not thinking about it?'

'No, one cannot. I am only telling you about it.'

'But you're speaking about it, so how can it be something beyond thought and reason?'

He flashed a rare, brown smile. 'I am referring to it such as a physicist refers to the fourth dimension,' he said. 'You know about this fourth dimension? Imagine a universe where there are only two-dimensioned beings . . .'

'Sadhuji, I've heard this before. Spare me.'

He was already a little past his tolerance for dissent and made an ugly face. 'How can I fill a cup that is already full?' he asked mockingly and shrugged at the sky. 'This cup is already full.'

These were the kinds of times we had, brief moments of argument, sprinkled amongst long, still moments of silence. The silences made the rest tolerable. To the mystery of why Mr Sadhu tolerated my presence and didn't beat me with his favourite stick, I had no answer. Perhaps I reminded him of a past version of himself, a younger, brighter and less confused version. But did this mean that if I didn't watch out, I could become like him in ten or twenty years? If I didn't hold on to reason's ropes and attempt logic's ladder, would I be lost in the mist and madness of intuition and confusion? I could picture that mist swirling through the heads of Mr Sadhu and others like him, sickly and yellow, and all around, and the ladder resting against a steep, sharp cliff, just about visible, and I'm running, stumbling towards it, clutching at a thin rope. On one side a thousand-foot drop, and behind an army of saffron zombies with yellow eyes and halos of yellow mist. Yes, perhaps one day I would become like him, chasing stumbling fools over a thousand-foot cliff.

* * *

One day Mr Sadhu told me a story. 'When I was younger, the world was a different place,' he said. 'Now listen, I will tell you my adventures. All of them. No, not all; some adventures. I used to travel everywhere, from south to north, west, east, everywhere. I stayed under trees and under bridges, drank from streams, ate whatever I could find. I did not have money; I did not understand it. So I relied on kindness, and the irritation of strangers. It was mostly the children who told their parents to give me something. I think they sensed my honesty, that I was no scammer, or king beggar. But I grew thin and weak and looked starved. I met many kinds of people, but there were two types. The happy simple ones, and the greedy sad ones.'

'Greedy for money?' I asked.

He slapped my thigh hard. 'Shut up. Are you not listening? Greedy for everything. They may even be greedy for happiness. Actually, the ones who are greedy for happiness are the worst off, the worst. They are so miserable. But the simple ones, they are happiest. And not, mind you, simpletons. Not the idiots walking around looking like robots, but the ones who don't want much.

They are blessed, these people. They do not want a lot, but no, more than that they want only what they have.'

'But how do you become like that?'

'You cannot. It is a blood-given gift. If you are like that, you will be a happy person. If you aren't, then expect misery. What's your name? Yes, Ib. Ib, you are not a simple person. The greed you lack for money, for things, for fame, you make up for with your greed for artistry, your greed for cleverness. You want to be the one who sees things that nobody else sees.'

'I thought this was supposed to be a story,' I said with irritation.

'Yes, a story about you. And about me. About everyone. We are all the same. But different. This is the contradiction. But once in the mountains I met a man; he was so sad, and so young. I said to him, "If you are already so miserable, what will happen in a few years?" He cried to me, tried to make me his guru. I told him there's nobody here to give him happiness. He said he had run away from home. "Why?" I asked him. He said there was a restlessness inside him, like his body wanted to run away from his skin. So he left a steady job, family and ran.'

'What was his problem?'

'I don't know. I told him geography cannot change biology, and that he was probably clinically depressed. He didn't like that and threw himself to the floor and began to kiss my feet. "Please baba, take me as your student and teach me how to be one with the universe." Imagine that, he's not even one with his family and he wanted to be connected to the Supreme Being.' Mr Sadhu laughed and took a puff of his beedi, and continued.

'So I took him with me, played along, to see the depths of his misery and lengths of his credulity. One evening there was a thunderstorm and we were in a cave. "You want some ganja?" I asked him. He wasn't sure but because I was smoking it, he assumed I think, that it would help on that transcendental ladder. So he smoked it very fast and started seeing things. Poor boy, the next day he was speaking about how an alien visited him and told him of his purpose in life, and the alien was farting loudly and carrying a bolt of lightning.'

I burst into laughter.

'Then what happened?'

'I couldn't go on. He was beyond saving, that boy. He was already so deluded and neck deep in wishful thinking that no amount of reason could have saved him.'

'What did you tell him?'

'I didn't say anything. The next day I left when the sun was coming up. He was fast asleep deep in the dreams of brahmans and energy circles.'

'Do you know where he is now?'

The sadhu paused and was silent for a few seconds. 'Ah yes, maybe some day I will tell you more,' he said, and no amount of pushing brought anything more out of him. He closed his eyes and we meditated.

* * *

It was said that the sadhu went back to the Himalayas from where he came. I heard this from multiple busy sources and it was strange that suddenly everyone was talking about where he was, but when he was here nobody paid much attention. It was the story that interested them, not the reality of his situation. But he was back a few weeks later and didn't say a word about where he had been, till one day he grabbed me by the shoulder and said, 'Come with me to the mountains'. Could I have refused? Perhaps I could have. But I didn't and with the curse of hindsight I sometimes feel it was inevitable, a manner of fate and destiny, nothing so grand as a supernatural plan, but more akin to the structured and robotic machinations of the many parts of the universe that is also our minds. The biology in us too grinds away as we are soft machines, fleshy and programmed, with terrible software and weak hardware. And so, at the mercy of these tender and fleeting fateful winds that drive much of our lives, I followed him one dusty morning with a bag of clothes and a notebook, almost jogging to keep up. He carried nothing, only a small purse under his robes, and worn leather slippers so thin, thinner than the skin on my knuckles. We boarded a train, unreserved, and sat like cattle, every man rubbing shoulders, the women protected by their men. At every station we got out and breathed in fresh air because in the carriage there was no air, only the sweaty stink of poor men. The journey was a day and a half, and towards the end, I was numb to the pain and the hunger. And finally when we reached, I jumped out before the train had come to a stop and ran alongside. Mr Sadhu climbed down from the high step, one hand on the railing, and looked around. We felt triumphant.

Onwards and towards the mountains one can only go by bus or car and we didn't have a car nor could we hire one. Early next morning we reached the bus stand, which smelt of garbage and where busses crowded together in large groups. The air was dangerous, with the constant shouting of bus conductors announcing their destinations. Families hurried along—fathers guiding the children, the mothers struggling to keep up, doing a strange jog made awkward by their bright saris—trying to find the one bus among the hundreds that would take them where they wanted to go. And it was dangerous because we were insects among giants, and had to watch out if one was suddenly reversing, and nobody cared where the giant went, only that it should rest in its place. We were lost in that land of giants until a belly with hands behind its back (in one local newspaper), wearing a red monkey cap and a sleeveless sweater, found us loitering and said, 'Where do you want to go, babaji?' Mr Sadhu mentioned a place, a name I had never heard, and the sagging belly, a half water droplet, was suddenly awed into a reverential silence for us daring and spiritual adventurers. 'Go to the last terminal,' he said, 'number 23. It's before 19, after 67. Ask, everyone knows.'

The bus was a scratched, dented, once brightly painted thing that smelt of vomit and pakodas. The driver was asleep at the wheel, his head on a bunched cloth. A few people already sat in their seats, looking up at us, on their faces that mixture of ennui and curiosity that afflicts travellers who wait. Mr Sadhu glared at them till they looked away.

Some of them namasted. 'Idiots,' he mumbled, 'fooled by the robe.' I found it odd that one so aware of the irony of a religious garment wore one, but I could not make sense of him anyway, so I let it go. Nothing in his life or convictions made any sense. It was as if he was formed by some haphazard coincidental storm of winds and lightning. But aren't we all?

We sat in the last row, next to boxes wrapped in jute that smelt like mangoes. The owner, a tired-faced man with sticks for limbs and thick veins, eyed us nervously. The sadhu raised his palm and said, 'Don't worry, we won't steal any mangoes.' The man shook his head gratefully and turned away to look out of the window. 'How does he know we're not lying?' I asked. The sadhu replied, 'He doesn't. But now that I've spoken to him, he feels more familiar with me and is comforted. Besides, I'm a religious man; we never steal anything.'

The bus started with a jolt that sent one box thudding to the ground. The thin man wasn't bothered. He was probably asleep. Dusk was shading the sky in a dull orange glow and a cold reached in through the window at my face. 'Better get warm,' said the sadhu, 'it's going to be a long night.' He closed his eyes and slipped away into another world.

When I woke up, my eyes were dry and a sharp cold wind rushed into the window making a low howl. All were asleep except the driver and a young man who played music on his phone. Outside there was only a thick blackness and a few lights glistened like stars in the distance. Nothing existed but for the road and the bus and the howl of the cold wind. I drifted off to sleep, and in my dreams there was an arctic cold from the north and an army that never slept.

The first sunlight was a hint of gold to our right that spread like watery paint. From this gold ceiling fell shafts of light like pillars that held apart the sky and the earth, like we were in some vast, majestic hall of old kings. Golden and thick, these pillars cast the long shadow of our bus on to village huts and dry rivers, long sharp ravines crowded with globular rocks, and as soon as the shadow grew shorter and we climbed the mountains, tossing and turning with the tide of the road, the trees, earlier so thick and full-leafed and rounded, turned suddenly to pins and needles and became tall and thin. Far away, beyond the deep valley carved by a great river, rose hunkering and jagged mountains, green and brown, silent and powerful, crouched and waiting. And suddenly beyond these green and silent goliaths, appearing without any warning, was the snow of the Himalayas, gathered in streaks, and embellishing the top of sharp and faraway peaks, even more silent, even more powerful, but inaccessible, priceless, decorated like special cakes, like powerful and famous people one saw from far away and looked at in silent awe. There, standing still beyond the moving green mountains, were the celebrities of the mountain world—the wealthy, the powerful, the cruel, the savage—protected and partly obscured by their green silent guards, so powerful and special that they didn't speak, one could not hear them, unless one went so close as to risk death.

The first sight of these misty, icy creatures made me gasp and shiver. I pushed my head out, braving the biting winds, because I wanted to get closer to them, to be one of the lucky few who are seen by the mountain, and not merely the other way around. But soon the road turned and the bus roared upwards through a valley of pine and fir. 'Are we going to the snowy mountains?' I asked the sadhu, trying to mask the excitement in my voice. He smiled and didn't say anything.

We got off in a small town and were greeted immediately by porters with donkeys offering to take us up to the mountains, but the sadhu ignored them and we walked quickly up a narrow street, leaving them mumbling and complaining about tourists. But my guide was no tourist and seemed to know this place well. I followed closely, noticing the ease with which he navigated the small rocks on the street that looked as if they were left behind by an avalanche. Soon we reached a mud hut with a thatched roof and a blue wooden door that was so small I had to crouch to get through. The air inside was thick with the smell of fresh tea. The sadhu said, 'Let's wait here for the night. We'll start in the morning.' I agreed even though I didn't know where we would start for or even where we were, but exhaustion had crushed any spirit of curiosity that may have stirred in me and I fell asleep on a blanket that was laid out in the corner.

I was awakened in the darkness by sounds outside, of shouting and running, and what sounded like a gunshot. 'Bandits,' Mr Sadhu said quietly. A small man was rummaging in a sack. The sadhu gestured at him to be quiet. He sat where he was and looked nervously at the door. Soon the sounds faded away into the night and we relaxed. The small man smiled nervously. 'Thanks to babaji,' he said and curled up in his blanket. The sadhu shook his head and laughed silently.

We set off early the next morning after a cup of tea and biscuits. The street turned into a rocky path as we climbed a slope and soon we could see the village behind us some way down. There were no more roads after that village. The sadhu, again displaying great agility, drew ahead of me. Ever so often he stopped and looked behind him, but wasn't bothered by the growing distance between us. The path passed over a small hillock and he passed over it and disappeared and for a few minutes I was alone with the rocks and the distant mountains that had appeared soon after we left the village, this time wearing special gold garments that they borrowed from the sun. I hurried on, not wanting to lose my way because I knew that would mean sure death. I found him waiting by a stream where he had washed his face and hands. 'Hurry up,' he said, and began to walk before I could wash.

That afternoon he finally slowed down and began to search the hill to the right, his hand shielding his eyes from the sun. Suddenly he quickened his pace and turned off the path on to the steep slope. We began to climb, using clumps of grass and rocks as support. And quite suddenly a plateau appeared on which he stopped. 'Aha, finally,' he said and his voice flew around the mountains. He pointed straight ahead and I saw to my surprise a large opening in the mountain, large enough for a grown man to walk straight into without bending. I was surprised because it should have been visible from below. Sensing my confusion, the sadhu told me to look down. The plateau that we stood on was actually a lip of rock that stuck out from the mountain face masking the entrance of the cave and making it invisible from the path and from curious travellers. 'Come,' he said, 'now you know where we need to go.' I followed him and we stepped into the cave. It wasn't very large inside because our footsteps didn't echo, but it was large enough that I could not see the far end by the light of the sun that fell through the opening. Mr Sadhu dug around by the wall of the cave and in his hand were a matchbox and a torch made of a stick and some old cloth. Light from the fire exploded into the cave and I saw that it was quite deep, and turned towards the right so the end wasn't visible. Once again I followed him through the moist passage and somewhere I heard the drip-drip of water. The narrow passage opened out soon into a wide and flat area. On one side was a pool of water fed by what I assumed was a spring, and a tiny stream led away down into the rocks and out. I was right. 'Spring,' said the sadhu, 'clean and fresh water.' He filled my bottle and drank deeply.

After some time of sitting silently, I spoke and my voice sounded thick and muffled in the quiet of the cave. 'Sadhuji, what are we doing here?'

'Isn't this what you wanted?'

'What?'

'To learn the ways of the sadhu.'

'Yes, but couldn't you have just told me?'

The sadhu rose and walked to the far end of the cave. 'Yes, perhaps, but this place is important if you want to learn,' he said. He leaned against the moist wall and poked around with his toes.

'So tell me then,' I said, trying to keep irritation from my voice. Even though I had learnt to temper my expectations when it came to this strange man, I felt the first pangs of frustration and anger. Had we come all this way across the country to see a cave?

'Make yourself ready,' he said, 'for this great spiritual truth.' He came back and sat down cross-legged. 'But first I must ask you, what do you think are the ways of the sadhu?'

'First, they have to be spiritual, meaning they have to attach in some way to the Supreme Brahman, the godhead, that which cannot be described. Then they have to meditate for at least four hours a day. All of us have that Supreme Energy inside us, like little flames, and the sadhu has found some way to tap into it and make it come out. You are realized souls, which means you know the spark inside every human, and thus can see right through people, either at their badness or their goodness. When you close your eyes you see the universe, when you open them you see the world. Moreover it is all an illusion to you, so you learn not to be attached to anything as everything dies and then you feel sorrow. At least this is what I have read.' I stopped and he was silent for a few seconds.

Then he began to laugh, a deep and full laugh that rose from the depths of his belly, a rich and contagious laugh that would have spread through a crowd like a wave,

113

a soaring and delightful laugh that grew more and more intense till he was shaking and falling to the floor, writhing as if in pain. I began to laugh too, and when we were finished he sat back up and his eyes were teary. 'Oh god, oh god,' he gasped, 'my cheeks hurt.' He massaged his face and his stomach. Finally he quietened down. 'It's all a lie boy,' he said, 'I'm a fraud in orange.'

* * *

A fraud? An intentional conman?

'No,' he said. 'Not a real conman. Listen to what I do. I pull people in, till they're drowning in my holiness, intoxicated by my special powers, totally and completely dependent on my supernatural tricks. Then, when they're my puppets, I release them, snap the strings that attach to their lives. How? I tell them I'm a fraud. Just like I'm doing to you now! You see? Do you see?'

'But why?' I asked, barely whispering.

'It's a scam!' he said, his voice growing in pitch and excitement. 'The problem is, you cannot explain to these people what is wrong with treating a man like a god—they don't receive explanations well. No logic or reason will help. These are people of experience. So I promise them an experience of the Supreme Brahman and instead give them the truth.'

'Why can't you just write a book or something?'

He laughed.

'They'll just go from one to the other, Ib. See, if I had just told you in the beginning would you have given up searching for Bliss? No. You would have searched elsewhere. In this way you have learnt a lesson.'

There was nothing I could do but sit and stare. It had seemed to me at various points in the time that I knew him that he was perhaps crazy, a narcissist, a liar, delusional, schizophrenic, disillusioned, ill or maybe just bored, but to be faced with the fact that he was an *intentional* fraud was almost too much for my brain to comprehend.

'You see now,' he said, 'why you shouldn't follow someone across the country just because they're wearing a religious garment?' He began to laugh again but this time cruelly.

I was too stunned to even be angry, so I only sat and stared at his cruel face disfigured by cruel laughter. When he had finished, I told him softly that I suspected he was wrong and misguided but not an intentional fraud.

115

'What do you mean you knew?' he shouted. 'What was all that about the Supreme Brahman?'

'I never believed any of that.'

'Then why? Why did you come here?' he said, now surprised and angry.

'I wanted to change you I guess. I thought you were a good guy. But honestly I don't know which is worse, an ignorant fool or an intentional fraud.'

'So you were trying to change me and I was trying to change you. How interesting,' he said, smiling. I didn't think it was funny and I told him that.

He sprang up with that same vitality that had so often surprised me before. 'How else will you learn, Ib?' he shouted. 'You are a pansy, a sissy, a credulous cow. The world is going to toss you about like a leaf, rape you and throw you in a gutter. You need to learn before it's too late that most people are frauds.' And he softened his voice suddenly and patted my head. 'You are a good boy,' he said, 'and there is a softness in you that will heal whatever it touches, but you need to be strong outside, so you may move about and spread that softness. Do you see?'

I cried. It was at once the nicest and cruellest moment in my life, and this strange dagger had gone right through any shame or defence I had. The tears were continuous and thick. 'OK, come on,' he said, 'enough crying.'

'It's easy for you to say,' I said. 'You've probably never cried in your life.'

'You have no idea,' he said angrily.

* * *

And so there was a lesson to be learnt, not in everything, but in some things and one must be careful in choosing what lessons one learns. Everything sometimes has the appearance of specialness but look carefully and you may see it's just a stupid coincidence, a chance happening that has no significance for you or the universe. The credulous see meaning in everything and I tried to avoid people like that, because if you have lived enough, you see that the world is full of bumping into things, falling and walking where you can walk, paths forged millennia ago by some unlikely force of history, of nature, of man, who looks out from the top of hills and decides on a whim to make a city here, a dam there. And years later you wander the earth at the mercy of those old forces here and there, at the mercy of new and old forces, and feel so special and chosen. I had learnt I was not special, not unique. Yet I walked freer and felt I had things to do, rather than wait for things to happen, because the special are convinced the universe will sort this or that out. I was an ordinary and miserable man, and was doing things as I had learnt, and what I had learnt is that I was a small creature in a large world, and yet could change it a little here and there.

* * *

When I came back from the mountains, things had changed inside me. I wasn't sure what had changed, but a definite change had taken place, like icebergs had moved around, some melted, some risen, in that cold sea that was my broken experience. And even though there was a change, it was difficult to spot and nobody could tell from the outside. But I felt hotter, and my ears turned red at small injustices. I tried being more forceful, to push my will into the spaces between groups of people so they would notice me. Mostly it didn't work but what counted was that I was trying. The sadhu was back in his temple—we had separated after our meeting in the cave—but he wasn't seeing anyone again. I left him fruits and chips occasionally when I passed the red walls of the temple. The peepul tree seemed older now, as if some great war had been fought beneath it and it was tired now and longed to rest. But I never went inside.

Some things were broken, some self-built crystalline structures about the world were shattered and gone, some clear things were murky, but others, once murky were gone.

The first few days I lay in bed wondering if things were a dream or real. I wished they were a dream, but I knew that they were real.

* * *

We had an aunt, a distant relative of Ajju's, a cousin of my mother, whose large white house was cool and echoing. It had lawns and a large jackfruit tree. Goose Aunty fed crows, and said they spoke to her. She loved animals but the animals kept dying of overeating; three dogs, two cows, till now, more to come. And she was miserable most of the time and yet managed to disguise her misery with her love for me and Amma. When we visited, the auto drivers would always whistle when they dropped us at the gate because from the gate it was a three-minute walk to the house. Amma was always nervous but I never knew why.

Goose Aunty cooed and welcomed us, her body shaped like a top, draped always in summery light colours, her skin like untouched butter. And she would feed us like we were starved; cream and strawberries, buttery biscuits, foreign chocolates.

But once when we went to see her, sometime in August, just when the flowers were dead, she wasn't doing so well, with a fever, a cold, body ache. She lay in bed, sniffling, sipping hot water. Amma went to her and pressed her small, cold, soft hand and she smiled at me. 'Your favourite biscuits,' she said and pointed to the table. When I sat they began to talk. Amma sat on the edge of the bed and nodded her head. Goose Aunty sobbed and sniffled. 'The babaji who is in the ashram near 14th Main told me to have two pieces of neem bark mixed with water,' she said. 'Neem and milk is even better Donnie,' said Amma. 'You know the Ayurvedic doctor there in Moshi Avenue? He said neem and milk is the best. Anything you have, crush neem in warm milk, you'll be fine.'

'Dr Aroop? I know him Rukki. He told me wheatgrass and tomato juice.'

'That's also very good. You know, last year I had a bad stomach, ask Ib, and I took it in the morning, just one glass. I was fine in one week. That's all.'

'That is also very good for skin, Rukki.'

'Yes, that's true, Donnie.'

Like this they went on for a while, exchanging medical advice and medical conditions, till a small Nepali maid came in apologetically with a tray of golden turmeric milk and Goose Aunty sat up, sending the bed into violent spasms, and sat leaning against the bedpost.

'Rukki, do you know turmeric milk is the best? My husband's second cousin, he had cancer, ya, cancer, imagine, and he was having this every morning. Gone, Rukki! In two years he was fine.'

They shook their heads in awe and were silent for a minute. The little Nepali maid stood waiting in the corner.

'What about that sadhu who lives in the temple on the hill?' asked Goose Aunty suddenly.

Amma said, 'I don't know, Donnie. Baba says he's a fraud.'

'Fraud? Oh my god, I don't think so at all. See, my husband went there last year once. That sadhu doesn't talk to everyone, you know. Maybe that's why Uncle said that. When my husband went, so clever that man is. He told him I would fall ill sometime next year—means this year, Rukki—and see it's true. It's written, I'm sure of it, in the planets. Tomorrow the moon is full. We must go and do a prayer there at that temple.'

My mother, slightly shocked, didn't have time to construct an appropriate answer, and found herself agreeing. So the time was set: tomorrow, 7 p.m.

'Bring Ib also,' said Goose Aunty as we left the room, 'it'll do him good.' I smiled and slipped out quickly.

I thought I ought to warn Mr Sadhu. Caught unawares by Goose Aunty could have deadly consequences for both him and her. And there was no stopping Goose Aunty when she wanted to do something. The priest had promised her, she said, that he would take her to the sadhu, that wise and powerful man who had predicted her illness. On the other hand, I had no intention of meeting him after our mountain adventure. I was still angry and bitter, my ego still stung as if a hot coal had fallen on it, and I could not get myself to see his ugly, dirty face. So I passed by the temple that evening and asked the priest to pass on a note. 'Don't open it,' I warned him, 'he'll know if you open it.' The priest was terrified of the sadhu, and shook his head nervously.

The next night we reached early and found Goose Aunty was already there talking in hushed tones with the priest. The priest was in his informal attire; grey polyester trousers and a checked green shirt. When they saw us, the priest disappeared into the temple. 'He doesn't like you very much, I believe,' said Goose Aunty as we approached. 'You know why, Ib?' I nodded and shrugged. We entered the courtyard and on the far end the sadhu stood ready. Our eyes met and I thought I saw a flicker of thanks but it could have been my imagination.

Goose Aunty waddled ahead quickly and when she reached him, fell to her knees and touched her head on the floor. The sadhu patted her head and said, 'Bless you, ma, bless you.' She rose and immediately began to remove things from her bag one by one: a coconut, incense sticks, some green leaves, money, camphor. In silence she placed these objects by his feet. He sat crossed-legged and closed his eyes.

Goose Aunty lit the incense sticks and began to draw a circle in the air with them in front of the sadhu. Then she began to chant, a shrill, hooting chant that rose and fell in volume. At first the sadhu sat still but after a minute he suddenly cringed and opened his eyes. 'Ma, thank you, ma, I bless you, may god bless you, may you live a long and healthy life.'

'Please bless my husband also,' she said.

'Where is he?'

'He doesn't like to go out, babaji.'

'All right, doesn't matter. Bless your husband.'

'Babaji, bless my husband with a long and healthy life, please. I cannot survive in this world without him.'

'Ahh, yes, bless him with long and healthy life, he is a good man, he takes care of you, puts food on the table, takes care of plumbing and electric work, bless both of you kind souls.'

She bowed again, repeatedly, and thanked him. 'This is for your health, babaji,' she said finally, before rising, and placed some notes in his hand.

'Please, ma, I don't take money. If you want, put it in the bowl there for the temple.'

Goose Aunty's eyes glistened and she nodded, speechless with blessing and specialness. 'Thank you, babaji, thank you,' she said and waddled away, and Amma followed her.

I remained in the courtyard. 'Ib, glad you came,' said Mr Sadhu, 'I thought you would never come.'

'Me too,' I said and sat on the floor.

'Shall we meditate?' he asked.

I nodded and closed my eyes.

After an hour, he got up and brought some tea. 'How have you been?' he asked.

'Confused, lost. Like normal.'

'Yes, that is quite normal,' he said, his eyes twinkling.

'You're back to cheating people?' I asked.

His smile went away and he grew serious and straight.

'That was her first visit, Ib,' he said, 'Let her come a few more times and I'll destroy her world. That's the only way, or she'll go to someone else.'

'I don't know about your technique. Is it worth the pain for them?'

'Look at your grandfather,' he said. 'After I rejected his ridiculous shrine, he just went to someone else and built a shrine. Now some fraud is making money from ignorant fools. I should have sucked him in and then spat him out.'

'He would have killed you.'

'Could be,' he said, 'could be.'

We sat thinking for a while. 'So have you found a job?' he asked.

'Not yet.'

'You know Bagram?'

'Yes, he said he would give me work.'

'Go to him, he'll give you good work.'

123

PART 3

SIX

I have always set myself up as an observer of things. I don't know if this is true, and possibly may be the other way around. But I ignored this little solipsism and maintained my place, at least in my mind, as the one who watches, a stationary thing in the midst of many moving things, a stick in the middle of a river, planted firmly by its pointy end in the real stuff, not the sneaky liquid that flows around.

Others pass. And in the process, I forget about myself till it's too late and the river is dry. Now a stick stands alone in a vast desert plain and not a drop of water anywhere. And if I was to take a little more credit and call myself a tree, say a peepul tree, then it becomes worse. The peepul tree dries, dies, is dead. This is the image which is most pertinent in my life: that of the dying peepul tree.

As I left home, I felt this movement in me; this same movement of others; felt myself sliding into the waters surrounding; becoming one with the flowing crowd. When Mr Bagram—whom I met first at the library office— offered me a position with benefits, I told him I could not do it because I had other things to do. And I was doing nothing, of course. The city I was lost in had become my home and my home was killing me with nothingness, but I couldn't join in because joining in was what made the city a giant killing machine. That was limbo.

But finally, I could not maintain this hold of philosophy over life, practical life, and one bright afternoon, went to see Mr Bagram, or Bagram Sir, as his people called him, in his office with a crooked, rusty nameplate and three flaccid plants by the door. Mr Bagram was thin—his face was thin, his eyes were thin, but his ears were thick. His face was always curious and eager and his smile emerged always suddenly, unexpectedly, creating a great stir among his moustaches, and it always remained a few seconds after its time and need, between thin, rubbery lips that sometimes showed flashes of stunning white teeth. He was very dark too and often slipped out of sight, into shadows, between shafts of light, and emerged, like a man made of the dark. From head to small toes, there was very little change in width: hips were uncommon, and shoulders spanned a great little length almost as little as the width of his feet when he struck his impressive pose. With an absence of those trouser-sustaining hips, he was forced to wear his pants just below his tiny chest: And here, quite close to his narrow face, they were held by a thin black belt. But when he stood, a great importance came about the room and caused the others (and there was always someone around him) to hurriedly stand out of fear—respect was the excuse—as if at any moment his height would enable his ready anger to smite them where they sat. When everyone stood, the height advantage rapidly disappeared and then they would try their best to appear hunched and grovel about a bit. In a room, this curious radiance of power from such small, weak quarters gave it a feeling of satire, as if it was part of some play and he would wave his arm to add to the theatre. What he did I never knew, but it was well known that he was a man with connections and was known to help people. He had many enemies too but always appeared to have vanquished them all yesterday with that outdated, out-of-context smile that he carried everywhere like a memento.

Mr Bagram welcomed me into his office from behind his desk with a wave of his thin, dark arm. The office was cool and dark and smelt of ink and paper. The phone rang and he gestured at me: sit. I sat and the others retreated to the corners of the office; there they stood, barely visible, but listening and nodding. He spoke quietly, firmly and politely into the phone. 'Yes, yes, I will arrange the meeting. But his office must approve first. Please send me the documents, then I will arrange the meeting. He is very busy, you know? OK, sir. Thank you.' He put the phone down and laughed loudly seeing my face.

'Ib, you don't know how things work, young man,' he said. 'This is how things work. I have connections, I make more connections.'

Then his laugh condensed to a smile and he asked, 'Can I help you?'

I told him about wanting a job, a small job, nothing too prestigious. He seemed disappointed that it was such a small favour. 'No problem, no problem,' he said and wrote something down quickly like a therapist making notes on his patient. 'I will find about this, Ib, but just now, from my mind, I can tell you, you know Father George Mathew at the church? You can go there. He will give you work at the library immediately. They have a very good library, you know.'

This to my senses was harsh because by then the respectful fog of religion had cleared and I could not bear to look any more at the details, which were rotten and moth-eaten. He saw the hesitation on my face and leaned forward from behind his desk (the others shuffled their feet behind me) and the many jewelled rings on his thin, dark fingers clicked on the glass-topped table.

'What is the youth of today doing?' he said (the others nodded). 'They are always looking for ideas. For these golden, beautiful ideas to fall like apples from sky, to eat it in your lap. I was struggling here. You see me? Any apple that has fallen on my lap has been rotten. I have become like this, of this much size, not because of my honesty and ideas and good quality but because of connections. Life is connections. Myself am not religious, you see, but I do go to the temple because of my family, of my life and my wife and my business life. I know what you feel—as a young person, I too was full of big ideas and I enjoyed till I realized, till I saw ants one day, in my college. And I thought, "These little creatures are so hard-working, and I am blessed with brains, yet I do nothing, just only waste my time." So next day I started my business.' He gestured largely around him to indicate his achievements and his kingdom. 'We must be like ants, Ib, connect, build. So we cannot be fighting, avoiding, offending people. We connect with other people. We form societies under societies. These days, nobody is teaching things that matter.'

'I'm nothing like an ant, sir,' I said.

He laughed. 'Then what are you, Ib? What do you want to become?'

'I am more like a tree, sir. I stand and watch things.'

'A tree? OK, a tree is a nice thing surely,' he said. 'We have many benefits from trees, like shade and coolness. But how can a tree move forward and grow? They need water and nutrients, and if there is no rain, the tree will die. But an ant, he will meet along with his family, and they will survive.' He stood suddenly and paced the area behind his desk. Then he stopped and said, 'Maybe you are a tree, Ib, but you must try to become more like ants.'

I agreed. There was no foreseeable end to the ant versus tree debate. He was more of an ant man, obviously, and I a tree man, and an ant and a tree, though of the same planet and DNA, are so different that even if they were given voices, they would find it very difficult to discuss things. Such was the case of myself and Mr Bagram; we were of the same planet, yet a world apart. But perhaps he did have a point, perhaps I did need to become more ant-like. At the same time, I was sure that he needed to become more tree-like, but this wasn't something I wanted to say to him.

131

'Where are you parents?' he asked, sitting once again and leaning forward. 'They know where you are? You look like someone who is not living with his parents.' I nodded and he seemed pleased to diagnose the disease.

'So,' he said finally, 'you want to meet Father George? He's OK, Ib. He's fine only. No problem with god and all. He will leave you alone to do your work. And maybe later I will tell your name to my newspaper editor friend. You like all that, no?' I agreed and stood to leave but he stopped me with a wave of his line-like hand. 'You always must watch out, Ib,' he said, and now he was serious and concerned, with none of that casual, amused affection with which he normally addressed me. 'Your face is very scared. They will kill you if they see you are scared. They will take you for a ride. Through the dirtiest streets, through the gutter. You have to act tough, even if you're not. Like a policeman. Your face is blank, pretend that you know what you are doing. This is what is the secret of India. This is India.' And the others nodded, agreeing that indeed this is India.

Soon, I began to work in the church library. The library was decent in every way that a library could be decent, and this wasn't something I liked. After all, a decent library means it doesn't have any crude books, and what is literature, the written word, language itself, without crudeness? That doesn't mean we are all murderers and should be, but in our deepest fantasies, our darkest hours, putting pen to paper: Who else is going to show us ourselves, if not these men and women of language and letters? And as someone called Augie March once said about death and how mirrors work, so indecency is the thing that shows us decency.

In-charge was Father George, a brisk and confident walker, with a distant hairline, like faraway trees on a smooth dark beach (from one angle), and a small, weak face. But his smart walking style didn't do enough to hide an insecurity that came out whenever he tried explaining things to people, which unfortunately he needed to do a lot. Sometimes, he would come to work late and just sit at his desk, staring ahead of him, like a zombie, or a stiff corpse, till someone knocked loudly on his door. Then he would jump up and begin his day, but the person who knocked would know, that one day if nobody knocked, Father George would be lost.

In a few weeks, the library had become home. I spent the whole day there, or in the large hall, till the maid shuffled in looking tired at six to clean up and weep about life and her drunk husband. I also began to read there, and despised how people interrupted: A young man, my age, looking for meaning, with a meaningless moustache and ugly trousers; an old widow looking for the Lord who, she said, 'buried my husband of forty-three years, then died with him. I must find that Lord again.' And of course, I found, god was not dead, but was indeed non-living and in that distinction, it was clear that god had never existed, but was longer-lasting and humourless like a rock or a plastic bottle. On a few occasions, science came, and was promptly thrown out by Father George, who had never asked for outrageous books about evolution and astronomy. 'Idisay

133

bad precedent,' he shouted at the disappearing backs of salesmen who, having hurriedly packed up their goods, dwindled into the thick city to peddle them elsewhere, in the same way they would peddle anything else, unaware of their monumental importance, of what it meant, small them near big church.

Some days I would visit Father George in his second-floor apartment. One evening he was doubting once again, and he felt very unhealthy.

'I don't know wadisthis illness,' he said. He looked scared, even in his own home.

'Have you seen a doctor, Father?' I asked.

He shrugged. 'What can doctor do for the soul, Ib?'

'Oh, it's that kind of illness, Father? Sorry, I didn't know.'

'Yes, Ib. Idis the pain of doubt. The torture of uncertainty. Idis the pain at night, when I wake up and there's nothing here in my heart.' He pressed his chest and his eyes grew moist with tears. 'I sometimes don't know, Ib, I don't know . . . Is the sky empdy? Am I a fool? Do you know?'

'No, Father,' I said. 'I don't know.'

'Yes, exactly, if you don't believe, then why it bothers you? Whatever comes, comes right?'

'Yes, sir.'

'Whatever will happen will happen, am I right?'

'Yes, Father.'

'But wadabout hell, son? What about punishment? I must understand it.'

He was silent, looking up, and breathing harshly.

'I will bray,' he said suddenly. 'Maybe I have some disease.'

That disease death that inflicts all of us, that strikes early, waiting with leering tongue crouching by the labia of our mothers, and enters through the fresh meat of the umbilical cord; then stays and licks at life; till finally it is dissolved and dripping on the floor of the world; and finally it dissolves with the heat from nature and the sun— you mean that disease?

'Father, you need to rest,' I said. 'You're too busy. You're doing too much work.'

'God's grace, Ib, god's grace,' he said with dangerous resignation. He had abandoned ship, this captain of sheep.

* * *

One day, sometime in October, Father George arrived late, at 11 a.m., and was distracted by things while he tried going through some papers. When I passed his office, he called out to me, and when I went inside, he seemed to forget and continued to throw papers aside, mark things. When the clock by the cupboard struck once, splitting the hour in half, he suddenly looked up and saw me standing where he had left me, and was very upset. 'Verry sawrry, Ib. You please can go now. I wanted some help, but . . . tomorrow. So much trouble . . .', and expecting me to inquire further, observed my face, and waited. When no sympathy was forthcoming (he waited only a moment), he began again: 'Nothing is clear, Ib. Everydhing is not clear. Why? Veerall just trying to live, right? So again I'm asking, why so hard everydhing is? You see this Internet? Idis very hard. Id makes everydhing superficial, so easy, right? One, two, gone. *Khalaas*. You have to work less and, but it does more! What is all this nonsense? So many mistakes I tell you, Ib . . . these modern times are verry, verry hard. In the olden times, there was no cheating, getting away with things. Now, Vobama, he just sits right, in his big office and one button, Ib, one button and people are dying. Dying everywhere.'

I said, 'Sir, he killed Osama but. Isn't that good for us all?'

'Good, bad, all right. Who are we to tell peepil what is good and bad? Idis god decide. Right?'

Yes, I nodded. It is not healthy to disagree in a church.

But I felt his problems: The way the old guard scrambles for new weapons. And he was no Janus, not even having one direction covered, confused and scared, finding that his one true path gave him the same rashes, the same itches that everyone else had. 'Anyway, what to do?' he said shortly. 'This is life only. It will go on and on and on . . . like this, till Jesus will come again. Then we'll see! Then we'll see who is going where!' He paused dipping into troubled thoughts. 'Ib!' he said suddenly, 'wait one minute. You come with me today? What you're doing? You're having some work?' He seemed to cheer up over the next hour as we took an auto to the other side of town by the bridge. He wanted to show me something, he said. When we arrived at a temple, he turned and headed for the opposite side of the road, where we sat on warm steps. I lit a cigarette and noted the feet going by, all dusty and dry, with toes exposed. I didn't dare look up at the owners.

'Look at these poor fellows, Ib!' he said, gesturing towards the colourful dome opposite us. 'See how they are walking around like clowns, and painting things, feel the colour and smells and what all . . . what is this? Some joke, circus? Nonsense! Is this how we treat god? Throwing things on idols, all false idols, I tell you. All false.' He was getting angrier and louder.

'Father, let's go over there to the shade and we can talk,' I said. He agreed and quietened down, and still boiling inside, followed me to the blue tarpaulin shade of a cigarette shop. Labourers, in yellow hard hats and dirty T-shirts, sat laughing and talking. One asked for tea but didn't have the money. The sun was inching over us towards the hard horizon behind, and it seemed to linger for a minute to allow us to talk. 'You want tea?' I asked Father George.

The dust grew from the road, raised by the walking and the loud cars, and the heat marked us down, on the back of our necks, through the tarpaulin that shuddered occasionally in the hot wind. As we sipped our tea, the light thickened, and finally after an hour and three cigarettes, we began to walk. There was a clamour of bells and chants that rose and fell, but a background of other noises—foul language, talk, various cackling discussions by the flower sellers who crouched by the side of the road—flew through the air like shrapnel. Father George was amused and smiled, enjoying the pagan misery. He left shortly after, mumbling and cursing. I was jobless for the day and wandered about. Shortly, the temple bells were in the distance as I turned a corner and entered a quiet road, a lane, under the bridge. A black river trickled by, obligingly, and it seemed like everyone had forgotten about it. On the far side, by the garbage-lined bank, a child played in the black water with a boat made of an old Pepsi bottle.

* * *

Father George was a creature from the past, a harmless monster from a foggy era of superstition and magic, blinded by the clarity of modernity, the sharp edges of technology and science. His face grew tired every day as the sky showed no sign of the god he tried so hard to convince himself existed. In that dusty weather he made his way here and there and saw nothing but reality, a reality he did not like, a reality of tyres and mud, sweat and death, naked children and their drunk fathers; and yet, he tried hard, very hard to believe in the fantasy of those black old ages, when knowledge began and ended in the pages of one book. That was an easier time, he used to say, because everything was knowable. And the knowable was pleasant. And the pleasant was god. And god was all-knowing and kind, master of flame and flood, and those who were naked were naked and those who were dead were dead, and those whose wounds were covered in flies had it coming and that's why their children bled.

And so it was verily that Father George killed himself on the 2nd of August in a small room off the coast of

Africa, where he was invited to spread the word of god to children whose best friends were flies. On the desk beside his white, bloated face was the King James Bible with all its pages torn out.

That whole month I had the same dream: We sat around a fire, me and some friends, laughing and watching as Father George danced around with a bottle of rum in his hand. It was a warm night and the stars were clear, and in the sky there was something comforting. Eventually everyone was asleep except me and the good Father, who twirled in the air, guitar in hand, singing the great songs of his time—Dylan, The Beatles, Rolling Stones. Soon his feet left the ground, and with a tune on his lips, he floated away into the night sky till he was a speck among the stars. But the tune continued and was all around. Suddenly my friend, the one with long hair, sat up and said, 'Such is the end of a good soul, in a bad place'.

I missed Father George. His confusion was a pleasant relief from the arrogant certainty of the stupidly religious, and showed an intelligence which, alas, was the source of all his misery. Had he been an idiot, he would have been happy, praying every night, convinced that god watched over him (oblivious to the rape of the others). He would live out his life blessing people, giving deadly hope instead of safe reality. But he was gone now, and it was strange the way he was so absent in the same way he was so present. The shock of death was just that: Like a current that jolts your body; the alive are so present and the dead so absent. It's the contrast that makes it horrible.

To continue in the library after the unplanned departure of Father George would have been stupid, and so I left the day after the news broke. But everyone was eager to know details, and so I stayed back the last evening to inform the cleaning lady and the other regulars. It was an overdose, I said, of medicine and alcohol. He had a massive organ failure. The cleaning lady didn't understand. All she said was, 'God bless him, ma. God rest his soul.'

* * *

After the end of Father George Mathew, I wandered for a while and did nothing. But soon I went back to Mr Bagram who said he had work for me any time. He had moved his business into real estate and could always use me. I joined him one morning at the old office (they were moving soon, he said), and he explained what I would do there. 'I'll pay well, Ib,' he said, 'ask any of the boys. I pay everyone well. We must keep in everyone's good books.' I was glad he was offering me a job again and wasn't bitter like some powerful men when you shun their first offer. The others said, 'He likes you, Ib, he's in a good mood after you come.' I wasn't sure why he liked me. Maybe in me he saw a soft clay that he could mould to fit his shapes and purposes. But this didn't upset me, and I enjoyed the feeling of being the one who brought good cheer to the otherwise glum and poorly lit office. Even the few windows that existed were on the wrong side and were grimy with years of natural dust and oil, so the little sunlight that entered had that quality of neglect, as if it was some long-forgotten tomb and even light felt hesitant and not in its best form here. Murali, a peon, who mostly brought tea and carried papers here and there, but who was also strangely sensitive to matters of lighting, tried to poke me towards asking for new windows. 'He'll listen to you, Ib,' he said one day, after placing a steel glass of steaming milky tea on my desk, on an old stain, so there wouldn't be a new one. I considered the suggestion, but then decided that it was too soon. It would appear like I was taking advantage of my privileged position, and that to me was the worst thing possible. 'Next meeting,' I told him, and he flashed a satisfied smile. 'Did you watch the match last night?' he asked. I shook my head and looked down as he began to talk about some cricket match or the other, ashamed that I didn't know what he was talking about and tired from the knowledge that it didn't matter whether or not I knew, he would still go on for an hour.

141

Those were the good times, when the real-estate companies had it easy and there were more new apartments coming up than number of people alive. And apparently it was a good year for Indian wine. It was suddenly Bagram Sir's favourite boast: Wine, after all, was such a classy thing, unheard of in these parts, but now being made not 500 kilometres from here. He had a friend in one of those companies from whom he would get 100 bottles every month, and the cartons would lie stacked like bricks in the corner only to diminish slowly in number. Nobody knew where the bottles went, only that nobody we knew was getting any. 'It's probably the politician guy,' said Amar, chewing his gutka, looking at actresses in a local paper. It probably was. Mr Bagram was involved with some shady characters: you had to be, if you wanted to be successful.

* * *

The following week I received news that Ajju was sick, sicker than wellness could reverse, and was in a hospital. It was the same hospital where Appoos was treated. So in the end his spirituality and religion had put him exactly where a crazy person went. And wasn't the whole point of spirituality to delay death, I thought, or even if that power was not granted to a simple mortal, at least make death a flowery and aromatic affair, without suffering and stinky medicines, and bedpans and shit? A spirited, holy, divine goodbye, with a background score of humming and chanting? A celebration rather than mourning because, after all, death was just the beginning? Nothing doing. In the end, whatever record you have tried to set sitting cross-legged and bearing the pain in the quiet domain of a church or a temple, you'll still beg for the ambulance, for a better hospital room, because the cheap ones smell of piss.

And so it was with Ajju, who, because of a contact of a contact, was in the suite, the best room around, with air-conditioning and a television and a constant corner nurse. The room Appoos had been in was way below, in the dirty alleys of that antiseptic city, while Ajju was high up in the princely castle.

When I went, Amma was there, sitting in a chair by the bed, and staring into space, although the window with a nice view of the park was not five feet away. She saw me and smiled sadly.

Ajju lay on his back, covered in a white sheet from toes to chest. His face was white and his eyes were open.

'Ah, Ib,' he said, in a croak, 'how is your work?'

'Fine, Ajju,' I replied and sat on the chair mother was on. She was walking around the room trying to arrange things.

'How is the crook Bagram?'

'Same, trying to run his business.'

'He's a crook, Ib, watch out. I have a feeling he's a crook,' he said secretly.

'Pappa, rest,' Amma said.

'Rest, rest all the time. These goddamn doctors don't know a thing. To gain strength, one must work more. That's what I told my men.'

His face fell at once unconvinced by his own words, suddenly remembering how old and how sick he was.

'Ajju, how's Silly?' I asked.

'Silly died last month, Ib,' he said. 'She was an old thing, my old girl.'

I looked at mother. She looked startled and had stopped folding clothes and looked like she wanted to say something. But the door opened and a young doctor entered in a hurry.

In a hurry he asked Ajju how he was, took his pulse, looked at a chart, told him everything was fine and left.

'See,' Ajju said, 'what a good doctor.'

If everything was fine why was Ajju in the hospital and why did he look so weak?

143

I took Amma aside and we stepped out of the room.

'Is this doctor good?' I asked her.

She shrugged.

'Didn't he seem in a hurry?'

'He insisted on this doctor because a friend recommended him,' said my mother with resignation.

I went back in. Ajju had turned on the TV, and was watching a documentary on World War II.

'Ib, get me a mango juice,' he said. 'Take some money from my wallet. Rukku, give him some money.'

'I have money, it's fine,' I said. But he insisted, and my mother took out a note from his wallet.

'Did you hear? Mango,' he said loudly again as I left the room.

144 At this level, the hospital was clean and airy, probably because the sickness and death was hidden inside air-conditioned rooms like Ajju's. The passages were white and spotless and nurses gossiped in the corners and doctors rushed past looking at charts. It was a different mission in this part of the building as opposed to the lower levels— here they tried to make the sick comfortable; there, all they did was delay death.

The shop downstairs had a strange assortment of beverages and snacks, but they were out of mango juice. I called the room from the reception and Amma picked up.

'There's no mango juice, ask him what he wants,' I said.

After a second Amma's voice came back, 'He says to go and find mango juice.'

'Amma, tell him I need to go somewhere—work and things.'

Again there was a brief silence and then mother's voice: 'He says these days even a sick man needs to beg. Ib, please just go and get it.'

I said OK and hung up.

The receptionist looked amused and said, 'Sir, there's some shop there. You can get mango juice.'

I thanked her and left. Outside, the sun was dim and the air was cold, or maybe it was just my mind. Those days things were dim.

A few days later, Ajju died, and nobody was in the room with him. Amma had stormed out because he had asked for mango juice again and the shop was out of it again and he wanted her to go down the road. She refused and he called her stupid and she was standing outside the room crying. An hour later, a nurse on her rounds went inside and found that he had died. The warning system had failed apparently, and they were very sorry.

But nobody made a big fuss. Amma was upset that she wasn't in the room when it happened, but other than that, she wasn't trying to fight the hospital or sue them. The whole thing was wrapped up and over, and what was the use of digging it up again, she said. I agreed.

The funeral was the day after that in the crematory. Some relatives were shocked and whispered that the colonel wanted to be cremated on the banks of the Ganga in Benares. But Ajju had told us no such thing, and we took his body to the closest facility available.

145

Ajju's brother pleaded and begged that we should at least scatter his ashes in the holy river. Amma agreed and said she would take the ashes to Benares.

Once the body was placed on the wood and set alight, Amma began to cry. It wasn't like she missed him already, but the sight of his old face turning to lava and ash was too much for her weakened mind. Appoos stood beside her, and from some deep place in his soul, had summoned a real seriousness that I hadn't seen in him for a long time. His eyes were upon the high, hot flames, and his hand held Amma's tight. He glanced at me and smiled with a strange sadness.

When the heat was spent and the fire smouldering, and the priest tired, the gathered people began to turn around and go home, leaving only Amma, Appoos and myself. Amma said she would have to stay till the ash was cool enough to collect. 'Take Appoos home,' she said, and went to the priest to ask about the technicalities of ash scattering.

Ajju's brother, his white hair plastered back, his trousers high and round glasses attached with a thread that went around his neck, came from his group and patted me on the back. 'Your grandfather was a good man, Ib,' he said. I nodded and he watched us till we left the crematory and went back to whispering things to his friends.

It felt strange after that; that a creature so powerful could dissolve into ash and have no influence any more on the world, even on its closest people. And maybe death was just the beginning, not for the dead, but for the people the dying weigh down. And once dead, the body sinks to the earth and the ones around are cut off and set free like helium balloons.

It was strange; that total absence of a total presence. The way all his control and all his power, so absolute in life, was so completely, utterly, gone. Such was the effect of immediate men, I felt, that their power and strength lasted only till the warmth remained in their body, and when the body was cold, everyone forgot about them and went about buying vegetables and underwear, haggling.

Amma went through the obligatory sadness, then, when society turned away to tend to other concerns, she was lighter, and though she didn't smile more, I could see a freeness in her movement and an independence in her decisions that I had never seen before. Without consulting anyone, she moved Appoos back to a nursing home, and began a knitting project. I visited her every day for a few days after Ajju disappeared, concerned, but she seemed in excellent condition.

I had some money, not much, but some, and with that I bought her a knitting set, better than the one she had. When she saw it, she exclaimed and thanked me but I never saw it again and found out later that it was the wrong type of knitting set, the one with short needles, and she used the long type, for better results. But it was the thought that counted, I thought, and was satisfied, I think.

But sometimes, rarely, aided by some chance music, old weather, mother would slip into a blank phase and turn away, perhaps remembering. And apart from that Ajju was never brought up till the day of the will.

That day, his lawyer, Mr Muthappa, a small, energetic man, always in a hurry, summoned us to his office one morning. Standing before his large desk, he looked at us over glasses and said, 'Where is Mr Surya?'

My mother said he hadn't come, that flights were very expensive. The lawyer shook his head and asked us to sit.

'According to General's will, all his assets are for Mr Surya. The dog is for Ib. But I think so the dog is dead, right? Yes. House, shares, property on Solly Road for Mr Surya. All other items, Mrs Rukmini can dispose of as appropriate. You are Mrs Rukmini, right?'

Apparently, this was to be expected, and the anger and shock inside me died away with a whimper when I saw that mother wasn't in the least shocked or angry. She knew Ajju would leave his property according to Hindu law; everything to the son. Amma signed some papers and we left with the keys to the house, to empty it, clean it out.

In the auto she sighed and said, 'Ib, can you go to the house and see what to do? You can take anything you want, OK?' She gave me the keys and got off near our house and told the driver to take me to Ajju's. The driver wasn't too pleased and argued. Amma couldn't muster the strength to argue in return, so she agreed to his terms and we left her standing on the road looking tired.

Without Ajju, the house seemed normal and small. The roses were in full bloom, too. And the bars were essential to keep the bad people out. The rooms were musty and still smelt of Silly.

It was made clear that the house would go to Foreign Uncle, even though it had been years since he had come; and everything in it, to Amma, the daughter, the one who suffered, trying to get mango juice.

Was there anything of value in the house? Depends on your position on value, where you come from, your hopes and desires, your dreams, your nightmares.

In the upstairs office, there was a drawer filled with old pens, all gifts probably from Ajju's friends and colleagues. There were pens with golden inlays and silver etchings; engraved wood and jewelled nibs; one made of stone and metal. They were all old, all perfectly cleaned, and in another drawer were the bottles of ink: blood red, sad blue, great black.

These tools were of great interest to me and I packed them into a shoebox.

149

In the safe in his bedroom, there was money, not much, but enough. For an instant I considered, then dismissed.

On the shelves, small square holes of stillness into the past, pieces of a life that no more stood erect and smiling. Ajju with soldiers and a background of ice and stone; Ajju and the President, a medal received; Ajju and his wife, confidence, pride, stature, and diminutive, traditional, a smile escapes, the thrill, probably, of being photographed, and behind, an anywhere street, a nowhere road, some trees, an old car.

Would Amma want these? In the hall, a piano, untouched, save for the pattering of little mouse feet on the dust on the lid. This would be worth a lot, I thought, and opened the lid, and punched out a nonsense tune.

Maybe enough for Appoos to spend an entire year in the nursing home. Tung, tung, tung, tuuuung; a new TV for Amma, tung, tung, tatung, a motorbike for me?

The unanchored notes gasped and floated away, not belonging to any tune, bounced about in the dust and came to rest in the silence, joined the silence, and it felt like it would take a bomb blast to lift this house out from its hole in the past.

And then finally I felt sadness, aided perhaps by those futile notes, by the dust that keeps thickening, by the untouchable past, the inevitable future, and by everything else that pushes us around. Ajju was also once a young man with dreams who sat somewhere and had a thought about girls, about a sunset in another country; and this was the sum of his life—a dusty house with a lonely piano and some photographs.

'Life is cruel,' I said aloud and the piano hummed and shuddered in response. It knew how bad things were; the piano always knows.

* * *

I had heard the saying 'Life is a crazy man's game' but had never taken it seriously because crazy people were very rarely fun, and this wasn't a light thing to say. But a few days after the visit to the lawyer, life, it seemed, was determined to be pretty crazy, unhinged, and surprised all of us.

It was still afternoon, I remember, and I sat with mother going through Ajju's old records, sorting things out, tying up loose ends when the phone, silent after a long time, shrieked to life. Amma looked tired, and she probably thought it was one more of Ajju's old friends calling to find out if he was really dead, and was this possible. But her face changed on the phone, from fatigue and boredom to brief joy, then checked, to confusion. She put it down and gaped.

'That was Surya,' she said. 'He doesn't want property, anything. He's given up all worldly pleasure. He's going to Rishikesh.'

Without realizing it, I had jumped up and was half way in the air, then when I landed, somehow I bounced up again. Amma laughed.

'Are you sure, Ma? Are you absolutely sure?'

She nodded in disbelief. This was excellent news to us. First, because we had no feelings left for Foreign Uncle; second, because it was completely voluntary; and third, because with Ajju's property and money, Amma could get Appoos the best care available. It really was the best thing that could happen, and Amma realized that and suddenly she stopped laughing and grew concerned.

'Should I have tried to convince him? I didn't say anything,' she said.

'Don't say that, Amma. It's his decision. If he's giving up everything, I'm sure he thought about it a lot.'

'Yes, but Pappa wanted him to . . .'

'That's on him. All on him.'

She allowed herself to smile again, then felt guilty and pretended to read something on a piece of paper.

'Means I can send Appoos to Angelou's,' she said.

'You can get a new TV too, Ma!' I shouted, unable to contain myself. I jumped about the room like a crazy ball, and briefly held her hands and tried to evoke a dance but she shyly pulled her hands away.

'I'll make some coffee, babu, the good coffee. Ask Appoos too.'

I found Appoos by the window in his room looking out. He had heard the celebrations, and was smiling too.

'Hi, Appoos,' I said and hugged him sideways.

'Ib, Ajju is dead. You know that, right?' he said. He was still smiling. It was difficult to make out the context of Appoos's expressions.

I said, 'You want some coffee?'

He looked puzzled.

'Coffee?' he said. 'Tea. Biscuits. Manatee. Pop stars.'

Amma was in the kitchen smiling to herself.

'You deserve it, Ma,' I said.

'Do I, Ib?' She stirred the coffee thoughtfully and then said, 'What about Appoos?'

'What, Ma? You know he'll get better care at Angelou's.'

'I know, I know,' she said, 'but I hope he understands.'

* * *

In May that year, we moved offices, from that small, dark room with grills and metal shelves to a shiny sprawl of a building covered in reflective surfaces outside and sleek wood inside. It was quite a jump up for us, and some of the boys were finding it uncomfortable sitting on the brand new swivelling chairs. First, they swivelled; and second, they were soft, and nothing had prepared them for the convenience and comfort. Ajit, the new boy from Mumbai, rejected this modern miracle and acquired for himself a metal stool, blue and circular, from where only he knew. Mr Bagram wasn't too pleased as he made the rounds one morning and made his opinion quite clear, stopping by Ajit's table and saying sternly but to nobody in particular: 'Some people will remain small all their lives and never enjoy life.' The metal stool was never seen again.

But work dried up for Mr Bagram. The real-estate market was in the gutter, and he began to travel more and look tired. The nature of his work changed; from sitting, it became travelling. From plenty of laughs and talk, it became hurried and silent.

I went along with Mr Bagram often, when he had no specific work for me in the office, on his trips out of town, but never alone. There was always one other guy who barely spoke and the guy changed every time. Some business associate or friend's contact was Mr Bagram's introduction. I always wondered why they spoke so little. But they were all right on journeys, and I was glad they weren't the talkative types who ruin every landscape. We drove mostly, though one time we took a train, but that didn't work out well because Mr Bagram found it hard to use the loo. 'When I think of my arse occupying the same airspace as hundreds of other arses, it is very troubling,' he confessed to me solemnly a few days later, as an attempt to explain and perhaps apologize for being on edge throughout the journey. (He had snapped at me when I asked him if

153

we were reaching before or after lunch). Never again did we take the train and instead drove his brand-new dark-blue Maruti Omni that smelt of apples and rubber. He was proud of his car and kept it clean. 'My first car,' he used to say, 'is the favourite car.' But that wasn't enough. He had to insist that it was also the best car. 'The other ones are not spacious, are not smooth,' he declared one evening when someone in the same building had bought a new Hyundai car, around which a small crowd had gathered. It was the first snazzy non-Maruti that we had ever seen. 'But Koreans?' somebody said, echoing everyone's thoughts, 'Are they good?' 'LG is there, yaar, Samsung also. They're very good companies,' answered someone else wisely. The owner appeared smiling widely and opened his car with the remote from a distance. As he approached, the crowd parted in respectful awe. Mr Bagram wasn't happy. For a whole day he was found pacing various rooms and muttering to himself. The next morning there was a bright smile on his face because the Hyundai was nowhere to be seen. 'See, already break down, this Korean shit,' he said to me when I went to his office. Later we found out that the Hyundai had been in an accident and was completely smashed. The owner was dead too and neither could have been said to be the manufacturer's fault.

Luckily, and perhaps due to Mr Bagram's obsession with driving rules, the Omni never found itself in an accident and served us well on our long drives.

One summer morning we left early. Mr Bagram wore a nice yellow shirt, and our silent companion sat at the back with some boxes. The sun was getting ready to shine, resting on one elbow on the horizon. 'What's the plan, sir?' I asked.

'Breakfast first, Ib, where should we stop?'

There was a brief discussion and we decided on a restaurant that was on the highway. That way we could avoid the traffic in the city. It also happened to be Mr Bagram's favourite restaurant for coffee and idlis but the dosas weren't that great. 'They must ferment the batter a little bit more,' he advised me once. 'Should I send them my wife?'

We reached earlier than expected, and the restaurant was just opening up. Steam rose from the kitchen, and the waiters hurried around placing glasses and spoons. Mr Bagram walked in and sat grandly at the nearest table, and anyone who didn't know better would have thought he owned the place, and not only the place, but every waiter and cook who worked there. But this tactic always seemed to work, and he generally got service very quickly and the waiter was always nervous and often got orders wrong. That day there were no mistakes. We ate slowly as we had been assured by the plump waiter, strangely unintimidated by Mr Bagram and his silent companion, that there was no hurry and that food was made to be enjoyed. 'If you eating fast, you are not getting the taste,' he said, with a plump smile.

'Ib, how is it today?' asked Mr Bagram as the waiter disappeared into the depths of the kitchen.

'It's good, but the sambar could be better.'

'Yes, yes, always the same complaint, man,' he said grumpily, but he knew like me that the things we hate never change.

With coffee, I needed a cigarette. As I left the table and made my way to the back where smoking was not frowned upon, I heard Mr Bagram explaining the art of making good dosas to the silent guy. 'You need to be spreading evenly,' he was saying, 'you need a steady hand.'

The posterior of that transient establishment, and it was transient to all but those who worked there, was quieter and more local, because nobody cares about the backs of buildings and what impression it gives. Without the style and structuring of the front, it felt more natural and was cooler somehow. I lit a cigarette, the first of the day, and sucked in its healing vapours. This was the best part of my day, when the first wave of nicotine made its way through my body and the morning air was cool on my skin.

The cigarette was finished and I returned to my troubled companions. Mr Bagram was still explaining something, waving his arms around, and the silent guy nodded.

'Ib, please tell me,' he said as I sat down, 'why are you smoking? It is unhealthy.'

I smiled helplessly and nodded. Mr Bagram shook his head and went back to illustrating to his silent audience the subtleties of dosa-making.

Business was always at the forefront of Mr Bagram's consciousness. There was nothing more vital to his mind. In the same way women were my muse and I would spend hours thinking about smooth skin and firm, flowing hair, Mr Bagram spent his entire life on some business deal or other, either in his head in the form of plans, or in real life. He was hardly at home, and I had never met his wife or family. That was a part of his life that he just didn't consider introducing to other people, and instead spoke of how much money he had managed to make on a deal that nobody else would have gone near.

That particular day, we were on our way to see his oldest and most respected client, a powerful politician of some sort, who normally stayed at his government-appointed palace in the city, but that weekend being a long one, was out in his country castle, in a green and coffee-covered part of the land, between hills and water. From the road, on both sides, coffee plantations spread their dark-green curls far, and amongst this deep green, tall silvery trees stood like sentries. 'Silver oaks,' Mr Bagram said, as if following my gaze, 'and see the pepper that grows on them.' He pointed towards the trunks where vines clutched and twisted their way up the strong grey wood. 'There was some near my house, where I grew up,' I said, looking out of the window, into the cool, dark depths of the wood and leaves.

'You need to go back, Ib,' said Mr Bagram, 'you need to go back home.'

I fell asleep soon after, and the last thing I remember was the smell of coffee flowers, thick and sweet, and the luscious howl of the wind in the trees.

When I woke up, we had slowed down. We were off the tar and on dirt. The car shuddered and complained over every bump and rock. 'God, hell this road,' Mr Bagram was muttering. Soon, we saw a grey stone wall, at least nine-feet high, that began suddenly by the right of the road and kept us company all the way till a tall black gate, like an attentive sentry who never left his post. Two guards stepped around our vehicle—they had guns. A few brief words and we were through the hard metal and into a landscaped and smooth world—lamp-lined paths, trimmed lawns, clipped hedges. Our silent companion let out a long whistle. 'Wealth has grown,' he said.

The house, at the end of a winding cement path, was entirely shades of red. The walls were brick with strips of red oxide and the roof sat comfortably on these walls, like a Vietnamese hat: two hats, one held up by the walls and another smaller one, half its size, floating above on four red metal pillars. White-framed windows punctuated this rust red giant, perfectly shaped rectangular windows that provided relief and character. Beyond the house were the hills.

We stepped out, Mr Bagram first, then me and last our nameless friend. Immediately, the cold nibbled at my skin. This and my nervousness were suddenly banging at my hand as one does desperately on a door when there's no answer, making my hand shake.

Mr Bagram noticed. He looked at me fiercely and indicated that I should get the box. Maybe giving my hands something to do would stop them from being nervous. I lifted the box and hurried towards the door, where the two of them were already being called inside.

It was warmer inside. Smoke from a wood fire tickled the inside of my nose, but it was a familiar warm smell and I was beginning to feel better, ready to tackle whatever the day was going to throw my way. 'Settle down,' whispered

Mr Bagram from the side of his mouth. We were still standing when the politician came inside from a side room with two of his people. He was a small man, I later realized, but an accurate judgement of his size was made difficult by the sheer reach and liquidness of his stomach. I had never seen the front of a man move with such mobility and with such volume. When he walked, it was as if some being—an alien perhaps or a large baby—was attempting an escape from his stomach, using the opportunity of movement to create enough up-and-down momentum to rip a hole and finally be free.

I tried not to stare, but my eyes were glued. With all my will I forced my eyes to wander over his entire body. His face was rounded and pudgy, rounded but flat towards the bottom, and his skin was dark, an opaque kind of dark, but not the opaque shine of African people, rather an opaque matte colour. His eyes, too, had a hungry look and were small and beady, hidden between fleshy cheeks and tropical eyebrows. When he moved, there were flashes of gold. He wore a white shirt, white pants, and by the side of the room, I saw his white glittering shoes.

He came straight to Mr Bagram and shook his hand. 'How are you?' he said, 'Have you eaten?' Mr Bagram nodded. 'Come, sir,' he said. Mr Bagram followed him to the end of the hall and disappeared down a staircase. I looked at the quiet guy, but he only looked ahead with the kind of expression that suggested he had no problem with standing in that exact same position and spot till the boss was back, however long that might take. So I was alone almost and put the box down by the wall, and sat down on a nice cane-and-wood chair.

In an hour, Mr Bagram was back. 'Get the box,' he said. I picked it up and followed him down the same stairs. At the bottom, there was a large dim room with a few scattered people. 'Put it here,' someone said from the other end. I crossed the room quickly, holding the box out in front. The air was thick with smoke and the smell of spilt whisky. It was one of the servants who had called out; I could see by the way he was dressed. He signalled sharply and I set it down. As I turned back to leave, it just so happened that I glanced into another room. There was a woman there, naked above the waist, standing in front of a large man who sat on a sofa, with a greedy look on his face. When I turned, the woman turned and in her face I saw nothing.

160

I hurried upstairs, haunted by this look of nothingness. Mr Bagram waited by the stairs and we went up together— he sensed I had seen something. 'Forget it, Ib,' he said, 'it's business.'

On the drive back, nobody said a word except our silent companion who whistled at the trees.

So it was clear finally that Mr Bagram was involved in shady things, conducted in the dark and smoky corners of the world. And this brought me face-to-face with a situation I never thought I would face; that I was working for this person who conducted such activities. But I justified it by telling myself that he was only a small player in this grey game, and not the leader. 'Like a soldier who must obey orders and play a small part in any war, just or unjust, cruel or kind, he too must make a living carrying some things back and forth,' I told myself. But this smoothening out of jagged thoughts didn't last long. Soon, I began to view Mr Bagram differently, without that friendly, humorous demeanour that had earlier helped me to fuzzy the bad parts. Now he was just a man in a dirty game.

He could see this change in me too, and seemed saddened by the situation. In others it might have brought out anger, embarrassment or just plain hatred, but Mr Bagram was only sad, and it was clear he thought it unfortunate that I had come upon a dirty secret, rather than troubled that he had one. 'It's business,' he said one day, the day before I left, and it was the hundredth time.

* * *

'If you are a stickler for the rules, you're going to have a tough time finding work,' said Major when I told him about Mr Bagram's shady dealings, 'especially in this glorious country'. He was on his way to the tailor for a new suit, because the old one was very last year in fashion and style.

This was a few weeks later, and I had taken to wandering again. Every evening, I visited Major at his new apartment and we had a drink, but that evening he was on his way out. 'Why don't you stay till I come back?' he asked, putting on a plum red sweater, dark blue pants, mud brown shoes. I agreed. Before he left, he pointed out the booze. 'Start without me,' he said and closed the door.

There was an amber forest of booze in the cupboard, different ambers, different heights, different thicknesses, and below, a stack of cigar boxes, cigarettes and a packet of weed. He lived alone, but he liked to call friends over and pretend for a while that he had company. But these were the kind of friends who never showed up when it was inconvenient or when Major was in trouble. They were the party predators, the sex scavengers, and only played the game of pick up and drop.

He was back in an hour, sweater glistening with drops of rain. 'Goddamn weather,' he said, 'Can't tell these days.'

He sat down and poured himself a drink.

'How's work?' I asked.

He adjusted his large frame on the chair and crossed one leg over the other. 'Fuck work,' he said, 'I don't like talking about work when I get off.'

I said OK, though I thought it was strange that he spent the largest part of his life on something he didn't want to talk about. But that was the way of the world, and I didn't want to probe lest I tear something delicate. And honestly, was it worse than being poor and unemployed, seeing things, observing things, but ultimately I was as miserable as the working people.

'What about you?' he asked after a minute when I didn't say anything. 'What do you plan to do?'

I told him I don't plan, but that the eventual plan was to find another job.

'Aren't you being a little laid back about all this?' he asked with sceptical concern. 'How are you going to manage in the future? What about money?'

'My mind doesn't work that way,' I said, but he wasn't buying it and laughed.

'If everyone said that, nothing would ever work.'

'Thankfully everyone doesn't.'

'What about some secretary kind of work?' he asked.

'Where?'

'There's this guy, rich bugger, used to own a bunch of companies. He's retired now and drives around fancy cars, throws parties.'

'Is he straight?'

'Of course, only girls around him.' He laughed as if recalling something amusing.

'No, I mean is he involved in anything shady, illegal?'

Major sighed and filled up his glass again, leaning forward and pouring it delicately.

163

'Ib,' he said sadly, 'listen to me. You're never going to get anywhere, never going to do anything without crossing a few grey lines here and there. And not because everyone is crooked, but because the system itself is crooked, man. You don't see because you're limited in your exposure.'

I prepared to counter his arguments, but quickly realized it wasn't supposed to be an argument, only a kind of advice, help, guidance. I stayed silent and filled up my glass, this time a little hastily. A drop fell out and Major stopped my hand and poured the rest himself and handed it to me carefully.

'It's a good opportunity, Ib,' he said, 'he's an interesting fellow. Has lots of nice cars. Didn't you like cars in school? You told me something like that once, I think.' He got up and walked to the window and took a deep breath. 'Cigarette?' he asked. I joined him and we smoked a cigarette each and listened to the sounds of the city in deep slumber, and the dogs were about, scrounging for food, howling and barking.

'On nights like these I feel strange,' he said softly, almost to himself. 'I feel a little distant and sad, melancholy, you could say. It's a strange feeling.'

'I know that feeling. It comes to me too.'

He put his hand around my shoulder. 'Remember college? The kind of shit we did. Nothing to worry about.'

I nodded. For him a time had passed and his life had changed, like lives do, in short bursts, then long silences. The place he stood in now was vastly different from the streets we walked in college, the night sounded different from this high up. But for me, things were much the same, the mapless, wandering idiot, poor and alone, a life stagnated like a sourceless river, an unfed sea, a rotten tree.

'I'll go and see him,' I said, 'your rich guy.'

He slapped me on the back and pushed me around. 'Great, Ib, great,' he said, but in his eyes I thought I saw a hopelessness, a sadness for me, and they seemed to say, 'I don't think this is enough. I think he needs a lot more. Poor guy, poor little fucker.'

SEVEN

Forcing oneself is an unpleasant thing, much like pushing a rock that is wedged deep in antediluvian muck, or starting a car with a weak battery. It takes all your patience, all your strength, and sometimes this is not enough, and one requires the help of friends and nearby people. And so I recruited Abbas, who owned the cigarette shop below, to wake me up on Friday so I could visit the rich guy, who didn't have any other time.

Friday morning, Abbas was at the door, 8 a.m. sharp, with tea and a cigarette. He came inside and sat down on the only chair, and I sat on the bed, and he stared at me for a few seconds. 'Looking good, Abbas,' I said. He grinned and thanked me.

'Mosque day, sar,' he said proudly, 'must look neat.' He wore a white skullcap with embroidered edges that fit well on his mild, clean-shaven face. His kurta and pyjama were pure white, and shocked the eyes in the morning light. 'Shall I go, sar?' he asked, looking concerned about whether he had done his job. 'Ya, ya, go, sorry. Take the money from the desk,' I said, pointing to the only desk. But he shook his head vigorously. 'Not needed, sar,' he explained, 'You can give me later also, no problem.' I protested but he left quickly, his footsteps clattering down the stairs, down, down and away, till they hit the tar outside and he was gone.

I caught a bus that was supposed to be the eleven o' clock bus, but it was twelve and I was getting late. I sat squished to the side by an old meek man who was squashed by another old meek man who was squashed by the thick arm of a large rude-looking man. The old man next to me shook his head with great disappointment. 'These buses are too crowded,' he said, 'When will they get new buses? Nobody knows. Am I right? These politicians . . .' And it was the same old story about politicians eating up the money that was meant to be for the public. 'That's why they're all so fat,' he concluded. I agreed with him, and asked him how many years he had been taking buses. 'Forty to forty-three years, I think so,' he said after some thought. The wrinkles around his grey eyes danced as he remembered the old times when there were only two or three people on the bus. 'I used to bring my son to the circus,' he said, 'but now my son is gone somewhere. I think Dubai or Qatar. But he calls often. Once or twice a year, he calls.' He checked his watch and adjusted the worn leather strap. 'Can you check the time, ma?' he asked, embarrassed and tired. 'My glasses are broken.'

I told him the time and he didn't seem affected by it either way. If he was early, so be it, good; if he was late, so what? He had nothing to do.

'Where are you going?' he asked. I told him, and he showed great interest. Suddenly, he shouted at the conductor to stop the bus. 'Get off, ma, get off here,' he said urgently and pushed me so I could move quickly through the crowd. 'It's a better route. Walk towards the bank, and you'll see his house.' I thanked him and he waved as I jumped off the bus that was already beginning to move.

But of course I never went to see that rich guy, and instead went about avoiding Major as much as I could, stooping in corners, hurrying through daylight and staying in the shadows. I could not explain to him why I didn't go and see the rich guy because I couldn't explain it to myself. Something that was obviously good—Why, then, did I not do it? One of those stupid and terrible mysteries.

And so I sat around again. And then some more. And finally, when my legs began to hurt from not moving (that pins-and-needles feeling, as someone once said), I began to wander here and there. I saw the city heave and let loose clouds of colour; I saw the city cough and spit out smoke and lights; and always those jerking, jittering lines of cars and trucks, and slower but more troubled, the people between; their hands to their mouths, their eyes disbelieving, their feet moving.

The cold began to come, slithering between buildings and under the door, making the tap water unbearably cold. Mist rose from the warm streets (the streets were warm because they carried blood) and people huddled like monkeys, wearing monkey caps, assuming monkey poses, seeing nothing, saying nothing, hearing nothing.

Ib's Endless Search for Satisfaction

Nobody came. For a month, I didn't speak to a soul, and my throat and mouth felt clogged and tight, as though the cold, like a cement, had seeped into my skin. And not only my mouth, but all around me, a cement was forming and hardening. Suddenly I felt that if I didn't move, I would be stuck like that forever.

So I ran from the city, to a school that Mr Bagram had once spoken about. He had said, 'Because this school is a very good school, you must go and teach there, Ib, because the childrens will save your soul and mind.'

The school was forested, unlike its surroundings, and was admired and talked about as an oasis, water in a desert. There were no guards, no great big walls, no cameras even though the campus was hundreds of acres across. It was some time before I spotted another human being—a child walking all alone and reading a book—to whom I put the question, 'Where is the academic block?' and who replied, through serious spectacles, 'straight,' and went back to walking and reading. Straight probably meant 'follow the road', and so I did till the road ended in an open and shaded lot, canopied by large tamarind trees. By the car park, a brick-and-tiled building stood modestly.

Immediately I felt this wasn't like the school I went to, in which there were so many kids that we didn't know each other. Here, everyone knew each other, which could be a good thing or a bad thing, depending on your brain.

Inside the building, it was cool and smelt of wet earth. The receptionist said, 'Mr Ib?' I nodded. She looked at me with disappointment, and then gestured towards the low sofas. 'Please wait,' she said, sadly, 'the principal will see you soon.'

The principal, a short man whose eyes always seemed to be looking sternly at his own nose, kept saying that he was a simple man, and I immediately knew he was far from simple. But he insisted. 'Mr Ib, I'm a very simple man. I do not like to create problems between my staff and myself. I am very respected as the principal.' I nodded.

'Mr Ib, I'm a humble person. I don't want to fight, I don't want to show off also. I received an award last year for best management. But I don't like talking about it.'

I kept nodding, wondering if he was ever going to ask about me, but I suspected he was the kind of man who didn't really care about facts and history, and more about whether he liked a person immediately. Of course, it was also very easy to be liked by him: All you had to do was never contest anything he said or, even better, keep nodding to every word that came out of his simple mouth. He weaselled on, saying exactly the things he said he never said. Then he told me that I was the first person he was interviewing for a teaching position because vice-principal Mrs John was on holiday in the Maldives with her husband of twenty-three years, Mr John, who had a surgery last year, and he had told him to go for a check-up, and that was what had saved his life, although he never spoke about it. I was relieved. If he hadn't interviewed other teachers, then nobody would have manipulated their way into the position like I was doing. He was saying, 'See, little things, I don't like to make a big deal about. I'm a simple person.

169

See, like when you entered, you did not say Sir to me. But all these small things are OK. You're asking, so I'm telling you.' I tried to interject and explain that I didn't know the rules here, but he raised his hand in a 'shut-up/bless you' kind of way. 'It's OK, Ib, doesn't matter.'

'Sorry, Sir,' I said again.

He smiled knowingly.

'Please report to our office person, Ms Revati. She will get in touch.'

'Thank you, Sir,' I said. He nodded, quite impressed with how he had conducted the interview.

A few days later, I received a plain white envelope informing me that I had been given the position of assistant English teacher at the White Berry International School with a starting salary of so and so and a reporting time of so and so. Please contact the admin department for confirmation within a maximum of two days, signed Mr Pacchhimani, principal. To celebrate, I chained smoke three cigarettes and drank a bottle of warm beer. Then I smoked a few more cigarettes, and in the middle of celebrating, I suddenly realized I was scared. I was no good as a teacher. I would ruin the lives of children and there was nothing more unforgivable—the fucking up was the parents' job. But from me, those bright creatures would catch the dark flu, the black soot that I emitted everywhere I went, that low mist that hung around me. Like me, they would slow down and stoop. And in that strange way, I ignored these portentous heralds and went back to my day of smoking and drinking. Thinking of these dark things meant tension and anxiety, and I had no time for things like that.

I was to start immediately, but from some chink of luck, it turned out that they had their summer break. That meant the school would reopen in two months and what could I do but travel and celebrate my new job?

And so I made elaborate plans, multi-layered and detailed, and the plans were solid till the night before I left, when I went for a party with Major and got up too late to catch the bus. With a rare hangover, I struggled back home and made more plans. This time, I would catch the afternoon bus in case of another emergency situation.

I left the week after. It was a warm day, and the bus stank of sweat and rotten vegetables. Sitting in that bus, nose full of the fumes of poverty, I hated not having money, having to suffer the ill-health and heat of the poor, while luxury buses swished past, enveloping their fat and sleepy passengers in cool conditioning and soft music. In my bus, babies cried out of disbelief for the transport that their parents had chosen, and their parents chatted amongst themselves of the new temple in their village. They would donate half their measly income to that temple and forego that doctor's visit for the baby. Outside, there were two kinds of things that people paid attention to: temples and restaurants. Both sucked you dry of money, but at least the restaurants filled your stomach and strengthened your blood. The temples were colourful, loud leeches attached permanently to that spot of earth where they stood and to the grimy money of the poor (and the leather wallets of the rich), but much worse than leeches, because burning down a leech as it searches for blood, reaching out into the air, sensing your blood, is uncontroversial.

The road was newly built, it seemed, for it was smooth. Some money had slipped through the dirty grasp of bathed politicians and had managed to do something, despite their best efforts. Red earth rushed by, punctuated by tamarind trees that looked like small dark mushroom clouds. And banyan trees, with their snake-like roots tickling the earth (under the vast shade sat locals selling coconut water).

Then came the forest—I could see the green sheet in the distance. From red earth, we entered dark-green trees and the scratchy sounds of men and women fell away and were replaced by the mechanical drone of crickets and cicadas. That sound drowned out everything else and the babies cried no longer. I felt immensely grateful to the cicadas who had no idea what they were doing.

In the silence of that jungle, many animals roamed. I longed to see a tiger swaggering across the road, or elephants protecting their young and trumpeting angrily at us pesky humans. I kept my eyes peeled, barely blinking as the bus groaned noisily up the twists and turns of the road, but no animals were mobile that day. Major had seen a tiger here once and he couldn't stop talking about its heavenly stature, its unearthly beauty. 'There's nothing like seeing a tiger in the wild,' he had said breathing heavily, just the memory giving him great excitement.

A little boy with oiled hair plastered to the side, dark-skinned, with large slow eyes had sidled up to the side of my seat and stood staring at me. I stared back till he left.

Finally, the bus shuddered to a halt at our destination—a hill station to the south—and the conductor shouted that it was the last stop, but he didn't have to, because everyone was already off the bus. Here, even though it was summer, mist hung low and people hurried about in shawls. Immediately, the auto drivers coagulated around the alighting passengers, forming impenetrable circles, which broke up only if you told them that somebody was picking you up. Then they muttered in disgust and wandered back to the back of the autos where they smoked and gambled.

Nobody cared enough to hassle me. I walked out of the bus station and down the main road, pulling my sweater tight around my chest. In the distance, I could see the hills.

A small smiling man asked me if I needed a room. I told him I had already booked one; where? And when I told him, he directed me. 'You won't see it easily. Just go straight. Dead end, turn left. But nice place, sir. Good luck.'

I thanked him and carried on past busy markets with cheap plastic toys and tiny medical shops. One man's holiday destination was another's permanent place of residence, where one had to go about their daily life buying onions and things.

The resort, called thus because groups of young people resorted to their most wasteful qualities here, had tents. In front of each tent was a fireplace. At night there were no lights but the yellow light from small fires flickered on the faces of the guests who sat around and drank and smoked.

From the darkness beyond the circle of light, a young man with dreadlocked hair sauntered towards me. He sat down uninvited and asked if I wanted drugs: The mushrooms were great there, he said. The weed was great, too, he said. The hash was great there, he said. Sure, I said, and he removed various small wrapped packets. 'Which?' he asked. 'Hash,' I said. He smiled approvingly, creepily, swayed in his seat, and performed the transaction slowly, till money and product was exchanged. 'Great, bro,' he said, standing up unsteadily, 'great product, bro. Enjoy.' Slowly he disappeared into the darkness.

The group in the tent beside mine shuffled uncomfortably and whispered things to each other. Then a girl came over, and I saw from the corner of my eyes, as she disappeared from the light of their fire and entered mine, how naturally natural she looked and elegant. Her hair was loose and dark and she wore dark-green pants that clung to her strong legs and a dark-green sweatshirt that was thick but could not hide the unmistakable bulge of considerable breasts. Immediately I was nervous but the hope that she couldn't see I was nervous made me confident. I sat still pretending to not see her till she said softly, 'Excuse me?' I turned and acted surprised. 'Hi.'

'Hi,' she said, pushing her hair behind her left ear with dainty, strong fingers. 'I'm sorry to disturb you. I was wondering if we can buy some of that stuff off you?'

In the primitive light of that orange fire her eyes were dark, but the centres glowed bright with hungry flames. Her face was covered in the most even skin, tight, and her lips seemed sculpted on to her face.

'I don't like selling drugs to people,' I said and she stiffened slightly and turned around.

But when she turned, the mists seemed to swirl, and the night and the darkness said to me, 'You fool.' And a switch flicked on in my soul and before I knew it I was mumbling, hesitating. She turned back to me. 'Sorry, did you say something?' she asked.

'You guys can come here and smoke.'

She smiled with relief. 'Thanks,' she said, 'you don't know how much this means to me. Those guys have been after drugs since the moment we landed. Let me go get them.'

I watched as she walked back with a spring in her step and explained the situation. There was some discussion and then the three others got up and came over.

They introduced themselves. Except the girl who had come over earlier, whose name was Meera, the two men and another girl were software engineers. 'What do you do?' asked one of the men, a tall and weak-looking chap who couldn't keep his eyes off Meera.

'Nothing yet,' I said.

We sat around the fire, five strangers, united by the illegality of some certain substances that provided unearthly experiences. Meera was closest, and I could smell her faint musty perfume. She had that quality about her, of calmness and reticence that I liked, and spoke only when she had something to say. Generally she sat silent looking up at the spotted sky. Soon, everyone was very stoned, and we were laughing at silly things.

'I'm a writer,' she said suddenly. We sat close.

'What kind?' I asked.

'Poet.'

'What kind?'

'Unstructured, unpublished.'

I was so close I could feel her aura on my skin.

'Tell me a poem you wrote,' I said.

'Feather fall gently/the salmon are going home/why do I fall so gently/why do I long for home?/The leaves turn sad/the sky turns sour/the men turn bad/the women go far./Come close friend/come from afar/let's anticipate the end/in some smoky bar./Let's discuss the world/from our tiny drunk spot/and be angrily hurled/into a confused lot.'

She sat quietly and stared up at the prickly darkness of the sky.

'That's beautiful,' I said. If she had turned she would have seen my eyes glisten.

'That's called "Smallness",' she said.

I sat very still, not daring to disturb the universe, and the universe was kind enough to reciprocate. The wind lay still between the trees.

She turned to me. 'What do you do?' she asked.

I stopped my mind and looked into her eyes. There, in the dark flickering of her eyes I saw something calm and soothing like a mother's voice. All my life something had bothered me, but her eyes seemed to tell me that it was OK, and that there was nothing to worry about.

I didn't want to speak because words were irritating and noisy. All I wanted to do was hold her face. And at once the past and the future seemed to make sense, and all my worries, all the discomfort stuck just beneath my thin skin, came loose and dissolved in the smoke of the fire and was gone into the darkness.

I tried to reply but no words passed my choking throat and a great pressure grew in my head. She looked at me strangely and cocked her head, drew her eyebrows together, and then she too seemed to understand, and she smiled and held my hand. Her touch was warm, and the warmth spread through every limb and organ, and I was on fire and I was alive.

Time was still; it did not pass any more. I was inside and outside at the same time. One second I was deep within myself looking into the eyes of my dark saviour, and the next I was witness to the scene from outside that circle of fire, observing my distant body doing automatic things, my faraway lips saying automatic words. Where was I? I was lost in a strange land, and only her hand guided me from falling into the precipice of madness. The ground fell away, and the sky cut loose and floated beyond space. Now there was only us and the darkness of the stuff in between, the dark matter. We floated somewhere between the ticking of time and the whoosh of space, held aloft by the rainbow-coloured strings of ten-dimensional space.

Then we danced and danced until the fire went out and the birds emerged and the first light of the day lit a small flame to the east that spread gently in the sky. She held me by the waist and took me inside the tent. Laying me down on the bed she slowly undressed, her body still swaying to some unheard tune. One by one she removed the rags of men till she stood there, clean, brown, smooth, multi-dimensional. And when she swayed now, her breasts swayed gently, and she raised her arms to her head, pushing her fingers into her hair, pushing her thick hair back, then pulling it down over her face till it was hidden, till the tips of her night hair brushed against her breasts.

She went down on her knees and crawled towards me and our bodies met in the first daylight. Birds erupted in joyous song.

The next afternoon I awoke with a heavy head, but a light inside, a lightness I had never felt before. It was a strange feeling, as if some primitive tar that had so far occupied a hard and tight place in my stomach was suddenly released, and in had come the universe, spacey, light, free.

She was sitting outside by the smouldering remains of the fire, hugging her knees, with her hair open, touching the earth behind her.

'When are you leaving?' she asked when I lit a cigarette and sat.

'Tonight.'

'Stay another day,' she said. 'My friends are leaving too. We can have a nice day alone. There's a lake we can go to at night.'

She didn't have to utter another word to make the case. Although school was supposed to start, this was a remote and unnecessary thought in my mind which I quickly shooed away like a stray cat. I didn't say anything but she understood and smiled to herself.

Evening came and she waved at her friends. 'See you at work,' said the other girl, then she looked at me and added in a threatening tone, 'take care.'

But Meera hugged her and said, 'Don't worry, Jo, I can take care of myself.'

When they left, she grabbed my hair and led me to the tent where we fucked again like crazed animals. And when we were done, I said, 'That was my second time.'

She looked surprised, then said, 'My fifth.'

When it grew dark, she pulled out a torch from her bag and we started up a hill. The fire boy had explained the route and any doubts in my mind were extinguished by her confidence and the way she led the way.

It was nine when we reached the top. She laughed when she heard me huffing and wheezing and coughing and fell suddenly silent as both of us caught sight of the lake and the stars in the water.

'Star Lake,' she said in a whisper, 'they ought to call it Star Lake.'

I found a rock and sat down. The night was thick with the sounds of cicadas and the occasional owl and by the

179

shore of the lake, the quite plop, plop, plopping of water dripping and frogs on their nightly expedition for food.

She sat beside me and for a few minutes neither of us said a word because once again words felt useless and inadequate and completely unnecessary.

She rose from her seat by my rock. It was cold and a dip in the lake was impossible. 'Just my feet,' she said, reading my thoughts, and in a kind of trance she walked towards the water and rolled up her trousers and entered, melting and breaking up stars and galaxies, shifting and liquidating entire worlds and their suns, and with just her feet. One could only imagine what would happen to my world if she undressed completely. Did I say my world? I meant the world.

The lake, container of the night sky, shuddered at the presence of this angel, but as soon as she stood still, it froze once again and the stars returned to their positions and the sky was back to normal.

'Come here, Ib,' she said, 'it's so nice and cold.'

'No way, I'll ruin everything.' And I whispered under my breath, 'Everything is perfect.'

The wind heard and answered.

She dried her feet and came back to the rock. 'Roll one?' she asked, but with those eyes and lips, it wasn't a question, it was an order. The one with real power, they are the ones who order without ordering. She had great power over me, that was clear.

With the drug in our blood, and among other things, love, she pushed me down on the rock and again we joined in the middle, met, melded, melted, and were done in a furious few minutes. Her mouth was still on mine when the wind suddenly became much colder and her back shivered under my fingers.

'We should go,' I said. She chewed my bottom lip gently and her hair was on my face.

'Going as soon as we come?' she said and laughed.

The walk down was shorter but more thorny somehow.

When we reached the tent, she stopped me. 'I'm going to sit out here for a while,' she said, gazing at the fire.

I said, 'OK, see you in the morning.'

She clutched my hand suddenly. 'What's your name?' she asked.

'Ib.'

'Nice to meet you, Ib.'

As I lay in bed listening to the crackling of the fire, the strange feeling of lightness was once again in my stomach. And in my dreams that night I wandered green fields and saw the mountains and the sky and the snow, and the woods were thick and silent, and all the time my right hand clutched the left hand of a woman, and everything was deep and good.

I slept the whole day. When I awoke, it was dark again and Meera was gone. Outside, the wind was chilly and the fires were already lit. But the fire in front of Meera's tent lay dark and smouldering. The boy, the lighter of fires, hung about and I asked him about them. 'Check out, sir,' he said, smiling. 'Here, she told to give this.' He held out a piece of paper.

Dear Ib,

*All I know is your name. Some things will never go away. Last
night was one of those things. Thank you.'*

*Unpublished poet,
Meera*

I returned to the busy city with a thousand thoughts. Why
had Meera left? Why didn't she leave her number? And
with every answer I gave myself, I had a rebuttal. Perhaps
she didn't like me enough to want to stay. But why would
she leave a letter, why not just leave? Did she not want to
ruin the perfection of that night by getting to know me
better? But that was a terrible idea and not one that Meera
would have entertained. Did she see my nose when she
woke up the next morning? These were answers I would
probably never get and I wondered, in the context of my
life, how long I would ponder these things.

At once the mystery and the unpredictability of life
struck me. How strange for this woman to enter my life and
give me such pleasure, what a blessing, and how cruel for her
to disappear again, back into her own life, and me into mine.

I had assumed an unconscious mission to try and find
this raw and fresh woman, because every thought of her
firm flesh, her forests of hair, was surrounded by a halo-like
glow, and assumed the unmistakable impression of being
the light at the end of something long and treacherous.
I had barely lived a short life, but there was something

conclusive about her, ending-like, as if even this sliver of time that my life had used up, could be meaningfully stitched up by this angel who came from the dark one night.

And so I made it my purpose to ask around casually—casually so as to not reveal my hopeless and romantic intentions—about her whereabouts, her life. Sometimes I swear I caught her scent when rounding an unfamiliar corner, and my eyes searched the landscape of ugly, uncoordinated buildings, and lunatic traffic, and dirt and dogs, hoping for a glimpse of her dark greenness, her dark shadow, her shadowy eyes, with fire in the centre. But there was nothing. Never was there anything but the hopeless city and its unthinking thousands.

Perhaps, it struck me around this time, that the thousands in the city, hollow and empty, were unthinking precisely because they were older and had had that experience, similar to the one by the fire, that had reduced their life to the pursuit of just one thing—love, money, fame, muscles—and it was no more necessary to think than to perform a dance, and everything was permitted in the pursuit of this one thing. Or maybe two things, who knew. In my case, the lack of the one thing, the two things, the three things, nothing, had infused my life with a kind of thoughtful aimlessness, an intellectual unemployment. And I found many times that time and effort aimed at one thing reduced the width and depth of my mind, the broadness of my thoughts, as if all my brain's energy was spent on that certain task.

With this in mind, this emptiness mocking me, I joined the school. Soon, I found that the school, despite its geography and trees, was like any other school—where the brightest of humanity are crushed and pressed into the dullest of circumstances. But a job is a job, I told myself, but the thought rang hollow and bounced around the emptiness of my skull.

A few dull months passed and all the while in the back of my mind, like a permanent mist, was Meera. I had still to make any attempt to reach her—perhaps I was fearful of what I would find, the reason for her abrupt and reticent departure. But one day I could contain myself no more, and with the aid of that freeing elixir—Black Label, soda—I asked Major.

It was a Thursday, and Major was over, drinking and smoking, his chest heavy, he said, with tension and anger. I told him about the girl. He was lost for a few moments, and then suddenly he perked up and asked her name.

'Meera,' I said, and just saying the name out loud tickled my balls.

'Wait a sec, I know this girl. She was in the publishing house, the one with Annie, the one with the . . . ?' he cupped his arms beneath his chest . . . 'the big ones . . .'

I nodded 'yes' despite the embarrassment and shame, and was about to be upset, when he congratulated me, and slapped my back heartily.

'Good job, Ib, your first is a real class act. She was fired from there for being too good. Basically it was that—she was too artistic for them. I've read her stuff. Great stuff.'

'Any clue where I might find her?' I asked.

'No,' he said, and thought for a while.

'Annie'll know,' he said finally, his mind slowed by the rivers of THC in his otherwise red-blooded veins. 'I think Annie'll know.'

I thanked him and was again struck by the strangeness of things, a strangeness heightened by the same ticklish stuff that had now driven Major into hoarse laughter at the sight of a solitary apple on the table.

How odd it was that the girl who had entered my body and possessed me was known to my best friend. But was it really that odd? Perhaps it spoke of how narrow our world was, how small in radius the circle of our world. I had heard people say small world, but what they really should be saying is small lives.

This dark thought, of the smallness of our lives, like the poem she had spoken, gave me pause. Suddenly I wanted to be in other places, but then I realized it wasn't sudden, and it was what I had wanted to do all my life; to expand my life, to gain the greatest degree of omniscience possible for a man to have. How could I know everything, be everywhere, meet people I didn't know?

I took this question along with me the next evening, when I went to meet Annie. She was late, as she usually was, and arrived with great pomp, waiter in tow (he held one of her half-dozen shopping bags), and with great pleasure she said, 'Sorry, Ib, I can't help being late.' I knew she liked this attention, any attention, and her life revolved around getting attention, even bad attention.

I told her not to mention it, mostly because it made me very angry, but she took it as a pardon and sat down. Immediately she ordered her drink (the same unfortunate fellow who had carried her bags stood waiting, mesmerized by this beautiful woman who had come in like a high-energy wind). He looked meekly at me, his soul already crushed, because he realized he could never possess her body, and asked if I wanted anything.

'Get him a small Black Label, soda,' said Annie impatiently, as if the waiter was privy to my alcoholic preferences, and possessed the same knowledge as she regarding my tastes. As he walked away in a trance, she shouted 'No ice' at his back and everyone turned to look at her, which she enjoyed immensely.

Once she'd settled down as best Annie could, she took a deep breath and looked at me.

'I heard some things,' she said.

'What things?' I asked, knowing fully what she meant.

'Come on, Ib, Major told me you got with some chick.'

I didn't say anything and she took that as confirmation.

'Who is it?' she asked, her eyes and face glowing with the pleasure that comes when secrets are revealed.

'Meera,' I said.

It seemed to me like her face melted. First it was made of ice, Annie was ice, but the name from my mouth was harsh heat, and her strong and solid face melted and was liquid and soon a dark puddle and in the puddle swam dark and dangerous things. Immediately she realized what had happened to her face and attempted to pull it up by the strings of her cheek and mouth, forcing a smile, but nothing seemed to happen. So she gave up and just stared.

'Meera from Rich & Coll?' she asked meekly. In her voice was some hope that her understanding of the situation was flawed and perhaps there was still some good news to be had.

'Yes, where you work,' I said.

It was clear to me that something was wrong, but ego and denial prevented me from inquiring any further. Quietly she took a sip of water and strained her neck towards the kitchen.

Like this we sat till the drinks came. She gulped hers down in three quick motions. I too took a large swing knowing deep inside what was to come, that the one angel, the one who melted over my body like hot butter, was a devil in disguise.

187

Now she was loosened up, her hair in slight disarray, splashed and waved by the hasty movements of her hands on her head, that betrayed a kind of desperation, and a conflict within herself, as to what to say, and further, how to say it.

Summoning some kind of courage from god only knows where, I spoke first. 'Go for it,' I said, 'tell it like it is.'

'I'm trying, Ib,' said Annie.

I lit a cigarette, and there again a cigarette was my only friend, my universe having been reduced to my immediate vicinity, and beyond that lay only darkness and murky things. The gravity of my life, the things that held everything together, seemed to be losing power, and it felt like at once everything would come loose and fly away and leave me floating in the darkness of space.

Suddenly she smacked her hands down on the table and looked me straight in the eye and her eyes were red and puffy.

'Meera died, Ib,' she said. 'A car accident. On the way back from some hill station.'

* * *

At first there is a numbness, always, when such things occur. Then the thunk! between the chest and the stomach. Then we look around, perhaps outside the window, if there is one, to see if anything else has changed, but the trees continue their merry dance with the wind, and traffic flows according to old rules and new haste, and the sky looks on with that wide idiotic smile. And inside, everyone goes on with their dinner and drinks, laughing and talking. Not once does anyone stop their activities, put down their knives and forks, or glasses, look with great sadness at me, that lonely boy in the corner, and come over, pat me gently on my back and say, 'It's OK, young man, time will heal all wounds', or 'I feel your pain stranger', or simply with a silence that words cannot fill, sit beside me and stare into the nothingness I felt.

For by that time I was alone. Annie had cried and left. She urged me to go with her but I couldn't move. She bought me another drink and paid the bill and left after giving me a tight hug.

And I sat there and again it struck me how strange life was that the woman who told me a poem about the smallness of our lives, had shown me how small our lives were, was now dead and gone, and nobody cared, in line with her theory of how small we were.

Drunk, but sober, I went down the stairs after an hour and stood on the road. The streets were quite empty now and I remember a distinct feeling of someone watching me. But the shadows revealed no shapes, the darkness no form or figure. The light from the street lamp glowed orange and weak and seemed to have given up on things too, as it stood strangely bent and tired like an old man. Not knowing where to go, or if there was any point in going anywhere, I stood there for a few moments that stretched to some longer moments and I was passed by a variety of odd people, some with crutches, one with a green eye that smelt of cabbage, a meaty boy who was screaming at a beggar. And on my right there was a tree on fire, and the 189 wind made it dance, and its hair was on fire, and the hair was a woman's, dark and thick, and I held it in my fist, and the sky had erased its silly grin and was now saying with her dark and misty mouth, 'You are the right person for this particular spot because you belong nowhere, to no one. Yesterday there was a man here but somebody picked him up, his wife perhaps, but you, you're going nowhere, no one . . .' And then George Constanza said, 'I like thick hair', and a salad formed from the remains of a dead body from World War II, red and stringy, with white crunchy bits, like a poem about death.

When I woke up the next morning I realized first that I was not at home because there was a cloud of the smell of food in the air, thick and buttery. Second, to my right was a shelf with a vase of pretty yellow flowers, some little plastic figures and a grey tin box with pastel-pink pictures of London. These were unlikely objects to be present in the house of one so morally and socially destitute as myself, and so I woke up with a start, like somebody had lit a firecracker near my bum, and looked around. The room was small and had just the one bed on which I sat confused but relieved and soon memories of the previous night began to run through my brain. But that instant Annie came into the room and looked relieved too. She sat on the side of the bed with a cup of coffee which she handed to me.

'You look like crap,' she said. Her eyes had a sad twinkle—twinkly outwards, but a layer of deep darkness below.

'What happened last night?' I asked her quietly, ashamed by the things I saw.

190

'You got so drunk, and did you have something else, acid? The restaurant called me and I brought you here because I realized I have no idea where you live.'

It took me a moment to understand and then it was clear that I hadn't actually come down the stairs of the restaurant.

'No, I just had too much to drink probably. What time did you pick me up?'

'An hour after I left maybe.'

An hour? I couldn't arrange things in my mind. Had I imagined everything while in the restaurant, or had I come home?

'You were asleep on the table, Ib,' she said worriedly, 'and you were saying something about dark hair, and . . . some other things.'

Memories again struck me and I began to sob. She sobbed too, and wiped her tears with the bed sheet.

'Sorry, Ib,' she said. And she got up and left, closing the door behind her.

It was the last thing I wanted, to be left alone, but perhaps she felt she didn't know me well enough to console or give words of support. I felt like calling out to her, but something strangled my voice, and my action.

I lay back on the bed, pressing my thoughts to other things, against the dark spectre of the job I was to begin the next day, but try all I would, there was only one spectre in my mind, the spectre of Meera lying torn and broken, blood and bone, in the midst of mangled steel. That same firm, musty body, those fiery eyes, and that thick black hair, and that voice like dark rum, were lying in a heap on some dark and lonely road, just lying there unknown for hours before the ambulance showed up and packed her pieces into a bag.

These images were too much for my sensitive mind. I pushed my face into the pillow, angry, tired, disgusted, and I think I made a half-attempt to kill myself but instead I fell asleep and woke up to darkness.

The sun had set—it always did, no matter who died—and the lights in the room were still off. A solitary mosquito whined and hung about and had probably had its fill of my thin blood.

How long could I do this? I jumped off the bed, turning on the lights, and wore my sweatshirt and went downstairs. The house which I had always seen from outside, was small

191

with shiny floors and complicated lights, and was quiet. I found Annie in the kitchen looking distraught but when she saw me she smiled.

'Dinner?' she asked cheerfully.

I nodded and sat down on a chair.

'How are you feeling? I called Major; he's coming over.'

I didn't say anything and briefly considered the possibility of leaving the house.

'Sorry, you don't want to meet him? I thought since he is your best friend . . .'

'It's all right, Annie,' I replied.

She sighed with relief. I had always thought her to be hard and efficient but now with a miserable person in the house she was on edge and nervous, lest she say the wrong thing.

I preferred not seeing Major because we were not tender, him and I, and the present circumstances called for tenderness, for kind words and intimate expressions. We never did that, mostly because of me, and the thought made me awkward. But at the same time I understood that I needed tenderness, and it was probably that thing, the comfort of blindly comforting words, that I had missed so far in my short and one-event life. So I stayed, and we ate dinner—chapattis and a yellow dal—though my appetite had left, and eating was like trying to fill a container that was already full.

Major arrived late. He saw my face and I could distinctly see his left eye turn liquid and melt with the lights of the room. Then his right eye. Finally he couldn't help it, and hugged me awkwardly. And thankfully he said nothing, either because he didn't know what to say, or he felt it unfamiliar—this tenderness. But either way silent affection, I have found since, is the best tactic to comfort the remains of the dead. Words are cheap and cannot enter so deep.

* * *

Months passed in that dull and dreary fog, and I walked, I felt, low to the ground and stricken-bent, like a destitute person, with no money or dignity. The world felt unworthy of attention. After all, why should one so hurt by his master pay any more heed to his moods, his movements, his unpredictable realities? The world was crazy and mad. It deserved to be locked up and studied from outside through glass walls. Nobody deserved this world, not even the worst among men, because even the worst are shaped and moulded by its crooked claws, from slimy birth to shrivelled death.

Of course I must note that this downward form was strictly on the inside, like an old peanut, with the shell, my outward appearance unaffected, but the real stuff inside shrunken and alone. And to the others with whom I rubbed shoulders—Annie, Major—I appeared almost back to my old normal self, which itself was always mildewy and low energy, and so they soon were accustomed, and thought me to be doing much better. 'He's OK now, time passes,' I heard Major say one day, when I visited him at his house. And I pretended for the rest of the day to be excellent, not just OK, to prove to him that his mistaken notion of my well-being was in fact correct, and in that way, I tried to convince myself that I was fine, by having others think I was fine. Obviously, this had the opposite effect, because the moment I went back home in the evenings, I went straight to the bed, with its unchanged and brown sheets, and cried.

You're perhaps wondering: You barely knew this girl, why the grief and despair? And to answer, I say it's not a matter of quantity, but of quality, and the rude awakenings from bliss to the sharp and crooked claws of the world. This jolt had a double effect in my case. Everyone has some unpleasant shocks—for a while things are humming along like a Tesla, seemingly driving itself, then suddenly there's a man in the sky, and your life crashes to a halt. And many such instances many have had; happiness, comfort, bliss and then unexpected events that bring sadness. But in my case, first it was the bliss that was unexpected, and to my mind, already tender with this shock, came the horror that cut deeper into this tenderness like a knife through a bullet wound. Or the other way around. Either way, the whole thing had left me pulped and smashed and thoroughly soft.

And the school? I barely recollect that period. I began to work a week after that night at Annie's. But hardly any memories remain crisp, and hardly any come back to me. But I remember the students who perhaps provided the few sparks and laughs that were needed to keep me from putting out the spark for good. There was a nice teacher also, a Mrs Aletty, who seemed to sense the layer of dank air between the shell of my body and the substance of my mind, an empty, silent gap, but she never said anything regarding this and spoke instead of our mutual interest, which was birds. I liked being around her, as she was an elderly woman with a kind and sunburnt face, and was always slightly more cheerful than you would expect anyone to be. And because of this quality, I felt balanced when I spoke to her because I was the opposite.

But I was never unkind. Bad mood, bitterness, hate of the world, and exhaustion at such a young age, does not in all cases lead to unkindness and revenge. In some cases it can lead to great tenderness. Such was my case, especially with children, whom I felt deeply must never go through unprepared for the horror that had so recently struck me. But how do I prepare them? I could by no means barge into their class and recount to them chronologically the horrors of history, going into the most intimate details of blood and bone, dead children, burnt animals. Nor could I narrate my sob story in song, prose or poetry.

This was vexing. And till I crafted that perfect curriculum, I thought I would do the regular stuff, from the books, and add helpful advice when appropriate.

I remember vaguely my first class. There were about ten girls and three boys. I was told to teach them English grammar, but instead, as I stood there, I felt an overpowering urge to make them understand things. I watched their expectant faces, which quickly turned bored. And I stood there blankly, with too much I wanted to say, and too much I was supposed to say. The doodling began;

195

faces fell and eyes were diverted to their desks and to the windows.

I opened the textbook; immediately I shut it. Then I opened it again. A girl in the front row raised her hand. 'Sir,' she said, 'what are we doing in class today?'

Her little face was still bright with expectation and suddenly it seemed cruel to subject her tender, curious mind to the sheer boredom of unchanging texts and musty wisdom.

I stood there not knowing what to say when suddenly my mouth opened.

'God doesn't exist,' said my mouth.

'All adults are miserable,' said my mouth again.

They sat silently, confused, amused. And suddenly multiple hands shot up.

'Sir, was Jesus real?' 'What about the Mahabharatas?' 'Is India the greatest country in the world?' Their voices rang with excitement.

I told them then that we will explore these and many other questions in the course of our term together, and preferably to not inform their parents about what they had learnt in this class because it would spoil their surprise at the end of the year. They agreed with great excitement and tumbled over each other and out when the bell rang.

The next morning, the principal cornered me in the main corridor and gave me hearty congratulations. 'Ib, young man, you are really a good teacher. The students love your classes. And to think I hired you without a doubt. The other teachers need to know,' he said and walked away, giving himself great compliments and encouragement.

And so this went on, day after day. The students loved the classes because their textbooks were shunned, and this kept the principal happy, and left the other teachers bewildered.

But after only a week, my ambitious project to liberate the minds of the next generation came to an obdurate halt in the offices of the principal. It was a Tuesday—I remember because Tuesdays have always had a strange bluish tint and the smell of sambar. I can feel now, as I look back, that bluish feeling, a little less dread than Mondays. The ten o'clock class was cancelled for undisclosed reasons, and I sat outside the school building nervously sipping tea (I was always nervous in those hopeful times). When the bell rang, I was summoned tersely by the principal's assistant and I could see in her face that I was in for a hard time (it was a look of evil mirth). But the principal was nowhere to be seen. Instead his desk was occupied by a kind-looking man with a salt-and-pepper beard and maroon-framed glasses. As I entered, he rose and I saw that he was tall and wide and was trying his best to appear less imposing physically. When he introduced himself, I remember thinking that this man didn't belong in any position that required disciplining, and for a brief moment, I let my mind ease into the fantasy of congratulations, promotions and prizes.

But it was not to be. As kindly and gently as possible, the director informed me that I would no longer be teaching there, even though the students liked me very much and were upset to see me go and had held a small and short-lived protest complete with banners that said among other things, 'This is a Democracy' and 'Listen to the Voices of the Next Gen'.

'Needless to say,' said the director, 'their brave and admirable fight didn't work. The parents went wild when they heard that you have been ignoring the syllabus. Mr Ib, how did you think they were going to write their exams in four months? What were you thinking?'

It wasn't like he was really scolding me. He spoke as if he was apologizing at the same time as scolding and his final question was more earnest than frustrated.

'Sir, I don't know,' I told him as honestly as possible, 'I guess I wasn't really thinking of their exams. All I wanted was to make them have some interest in what was going on. They're just children, sir. They don't deserve to be bored. There's plenty of time for that later.'

The director lifted his head and watched the ceiling for a few seconds.

'Then perhaps this is not the school for you, Ib,' he said, and he lowered his deep, kind eyes to my face and he seemed to be examining my eyes for something. I have felt this situation many times before and after, when people seemed to be searching my face for something that they thought was there, but maybe it wasn't.

I left the office strangely relieved. It felt like the director's final objection to my weak argument was more advice than correction and I was encouraged. Maybe I wasn't a bad teacher but a different kind of teacher?

I went back home and it was raining the pleasant kind of rain that happens on pleasant days. Suddenly I felt an expert on matters relating to children, and now being an expert, a deep sense of dread and foreboding entered my abdomen and refused to leave. I felt fear for the next generation, and a sense of tragedy pervaded all my thinking. Everywhere I saw children, a dark fog descended and I couldn't help picturing them packed into their buses and buildings like worms, even if at the time they were playing in a park or cycling around.

That evening I called Major and told him my troubles. 'This is not the way to live,' he said, and through the static I could feel his irritation, as if he had told a thousand people the same thing. 'You can't let some idea colour how you look at the world. It must be the other way around. Can't you see how the children play in the park, how happy they are? Proceed from there.'

But isn't everything we see coloured by who we are? 'Yes, that's why we should at least try to resist the natural tints of our species, of our family, of our friends, and try to be reasonable.'

I felt, when I hung up the phone, that it was much easier said than done. After all, it was only time, or so I had heard, that could blow away this dark fog that had entered my mind and lay like a blanket over every thought and every experience, and no amount of reason could chase it away and let the light back in. The dark fog was Meera's death, of course, and even though it had been a few months, that pain lingered, like an anchor attached to the inside of my stomach, pulling me down and low.

That was the first night I felt completely hopeless. Not sad, or sorrowful, or depressed, but utterly hopeless, as if the whole world was packed with cement and I was stuck at the bottom, not able to move, not able to breathe. When I contemplated life, it seemed absurdly short and pointless: You are born, you die. And the parts in between, the parts that were meant to matter, were too hard to change, too violent to take a walk, too noisy to sleep, too boring to stay awake, too complicated to ponder and too stingy to have money. All the people were robots, programmed to feel unprogrammed, so they thought they were important and perfect, and carried on, and on their shoulders (designed to carry so much), they carried the sick and rotten world, forever and ever.

This distinct feeling, that the world was on autopilot, went with me everywhere. People seemed inhuman, walking on fixed paths that were unmarked, lest the whole trick was given away and one of them stopped, looked down, and asked, 'What the hell am I doing here?'

And what the hell was I doing there? Was I any better? I had begun to drink regularly, wandering from home to the bar, and wandering back, a cigarette in hand, every night. On the weekends I went to parties and touched every woman I could, rubbed against every warm female body available. Major was worried and I could see him watching me, brow knitted, instead of dancing or smoking, but I didn't care, even though he was my best and only friend. Such was the depth of my nihilism brought about by my sudden awakening to the cruelness of planet earth.

How old was I? Old enough to die. But old enough to live again. Yet I lacked the energy, the inner upward gravity to stand up and throw away the cigarette and get strong, get fast, get smart. My body sat crumpled on the couch, lungs full of smoke and glass full of whisky, not in possession of a single good faculty, not one good quality that could make me live again. After a while, everything became the same: Wherever I was, there was a cigarette in one hand and a drink in the other, and the places this wasn't possible I avoided as best I could. And so it became impossible to buy fruits or go to the supermarket for anything. I relied on my friend Javed to bring me Maggi, and when he came in, I pretended to be sober and working hard on a project. It's funny when I think of it now: I had the energy to pretend to be OK, but not the force to even begin to get OK. Perhaps there is a use to bothering about what other people think.

My house, meanwhile, had turned into a collection of things that had only one thing in common: grime. The kitchen counter, once a nice, shiny black-marble slab, was a battlefield of spent bananas and dead cigarettes, bones, bloody plates, opaque pools of unidentifiable liquids in containers that had long since changed colour. And the smell: that sour, violent stench of old food and hopeless piles of dishes that I had somehow become used to. Every day there was a new fungus: first green, then yellow, and even pink. Eventually, the smell was too much and I locked the kitchen door and stowed the key. Actually, it wasn't even that. The reason I locked it was I couldn't use it any more: every square foot was covered.

I did my best to keep Major and Annie from visiting, having that much sanity and self-awareness to realize they would probably call the mental hospital. I knew they were worried because every day one of them would call, pretending they didn't know the other was calling too, and ask nonchalantly if they could come over and chill. Every day I made up a new excuse: at first, valid and believable things such as 'I'm looking for a job' or 'I'm going to pay the electricity bill' and then over time more and more ridiculous ones like 'I got a job' or 'I need to conduct research on the relation between poverty and football skills'. Even I knew they were stupid, but such was the desperation that now drove my life that nothing mattered except that my best friends never see what I had become.

One day, a few weeks since the kitchen was out of bounds for humans, Major knocked at my door in the morning. He had had enough and shouted, 'Ib, I can hear you inside. Just open the fucking door or I'll break it open.' He banged on it a couple more times, and just when he was taking a run-up (or so I thought) to charge at it, I opened it. He looked relieved and massaged his shoulder unconsciously. 'What the fuck?' he said, and he was angry and relieved at the same time. I called him inside but he stopped and said again, 'What the fuck, man?'

I told him I was sorry, that I wasn't free. 'No, what the fuck is that smell?'

Already he was tracking the source to the kitchen. 'Did you lock it?' he asked after trying the door.

I nodded.

'Where's the key?'

'Forget it, Major. Listen, man, I'll sort it out,' I said, rising and going towards him to escort him out, but he stood firm and his face changed to pure anger.

'Keys,' he said through his nostrils.

I got the keys and turned around as he opened the door. After the sound of the scuttling of rats, there was silence. I went and sat down on the sofa and lit a cigarette. I could hear him calling someone over the phone, then he came back out.

'Give me one,' he said.

We sat smoking, and after a while, Major coughed and went out. 'I can't stand the smell, Ib. Let's go down and wait. The cleaners are coming.'

On the street, the heavy heat and dry dust were a welcome feeling, and the open space stretched our lungs out. We bought some tea from Javed who looked relieved that I had come with someone instead of alone. He smiled and saluted Major, who was too preoccupied.

'What's going on?' he asked me.

I shrugged and couldn't speak.

'You know what I feel?' I said after a period of silence. 'I feel like all life is pointless. The only thing that really matters is sex. And death.'

He shrugged as if he'd heard it all before from the mouths of babes. 'Nihilism and hedonism. A dangerous combination,' he said, 'perfectly lethal combination.'

Of course it was perfectly lethal, because it was killing me, and I was almost dead.

'What you going to do?' he asked.

'Go away.'

'Where?'

'Anywhere.'

'As far away as possible?' he asked.

I nodded and looked into the dust in the distance.

'This country, man, this country is too cruel, too hard for a coward like me.'

Major put his large hand on my shoulder. 'You're not a coward, Ib,' he said, 'You're just too sensitive, like a Richter scale that registers footsteps. Your brain goes off in alarm all the time. You have to toughen up. I've told you so many times.'

'It's too sad, it's too tough, it's pointless . . .' My words were caught in my throat and I couldn't speak.

Major stood quietly by my side, and then finally he said, 'Go away to America, or Europe. You'll see how things there are bad in different ways. This is the way the world works, Ib, maybe you'll learn to love your home when you're far from it. Maybe it'll do you some good.'

Major, with his kind and soft heart, had turned emotional that evening, and we drank and smoked till the sounds of traffic faded and were replaced by the howls and barks of homeless dogs.

The next morning, he hugged me tight.

'I'll get you your visa, Ib. What about tickets?'

'No, I can't go away,' I said. 'I'll never forgive myself for running away.'

He smiled and shrugged.

'Do your best, Ib,' he said. 'It doesn't matter where you are finally.'

Now I smiled and shrugged.

'I think I'll go see Mom and Dad. I haven't seen them in years anyway.'

'Years? Really?'

Yes, it had been years, and I felt it in my blood and bones, this vacuum between sons and mothers. And maybe the vacuum had become too strong, the deeps too dark, to fill even partially, and maybe that darkness would suck us in, this one last time we met, and destroy us both. But that was a chance I had to take. Nature commanded so.

Major was watching me carefully. Then he gave me a side hug and left.

* * *

It was one of those mornings when the emptiness of the city was most apparent, though filled with such lofty stuffings. The smoke and dirt rose earlier than the sun, and when the sun did come up, there was nothing much for it to do, because ordinary light was no match for this muck and madness. The lane of my childhood was unchanged, as if the day I had left, everything had stopped growing, or, the society had hired a gardener to trim the plants, which was more likely. Between those tall silver oaks I could see patches of blue sky, but not enough to cheer me up. I made my way down the street and then stood in front of my house for a few minutes, unable to move.

There I was, returned to the place of my stunted growth, returned to the people of my childhood misery, after having grown out of blaming them, and now recognizing that they had very little to do with what I was, what I am, and rather than making me look forward to meeting them, the realization dawned quickly that, not being responsible for the misery of my life made them less and not more important to me. Suddenly as I stood there, I felt them to be strangers, and at once the guilt and slight love fell away and I felt free and happy. 'Why shouldn't I meet the people whom I knew briefly as a child?' I thought to myself. Perhaps they would see what I had become and feel the guilt and regret that I had felt for so long. In this lonely, handicapped part of the world, the two people who had given me birth were still tiny and walked about very little, and the reach of their arms was so short that not even their neighbours knew very much about them.

Feeling thus superior and triumphant, I knocked on the door. It was the same cheap wood, the same faux-brick facade and I felt a deep disgust with where I stood.

Mother, older, greyer, with the same nice face, opened the door and we stood there looking at each other. At that moment, the previous ten minutes were nothing, and I began to cry. And so did mother. But we didn't hug, no, not even then. She called me inside, sobbing and wiping her mildly weathered face. She was also slightly bent, like a tree for whom the weight of the atmosphere was too much to bear.

Once again, words were no match for the moment. We sat on the same maroon sofa and she brought me coffee in the same small steel glass. Finally, swallowing the grief and regret of years, I asked if Appoos was around. She began to sob again and she crumpled like a sheet of paper on to the sofa. I touched her back awkwardly.

Between sobs she told me that Appoos was much worse now and he could barely talk sense.

'Where is he?' I asked.

She pointed upstairs. 'Your room,' she said. 'It's the only room in which he doesn't scream.'

I left her crying on the sofa and went upstairs. The door to my room was ajar and I could see Appoos sitting on the edge of the bed. He was talking to himself, and when I entered, he didn't even notice. The room had changed; the walls were plastered with drawings I had done as a child and the cupboards were missing. Appoos, it seemed, was having a conversation with somebody about Mother Teresa.

'And yet she had the best care, and yet she never ate the same food. And the needles, reused needles, you think she used those on herself. Where did the money go? Saint, my arse, more like a god's personal thief . . .'

'Appoos,' I called out.

He looked up straight into my face and he said, 'Somebody sounds just like my little Ib today. Who is it?'

I said, 'It's me, Ib.'

'I know it's you,' he said rudely, 'but who is it really? Machupichu, is it you?'

I sat down next to him but he continued to stare towards the door where I was standing.

'Appoos, Appoos,' I said, and nudged his shoulder and then I saw a tear roll down his left cheek and he was silent then.

'My little Ib,' he said softly to himself, 'my little Ib went away to a volcano and never came back. Please don't be Ib, be someone else today.'

I hugged him from the side, putting my face on his shoulder. But he shook me off and complained to his friends that it was hot that day.

When I left, closing the door softly behind me, Appoos was laughing, and for an instant I thought he caught my eye but it was nothing. I stood outside for a few minutes and went downstairs.

Mother had made some chips and sat at the table waiting.

'Now will you go away again?' she asked.

I nodded.

'Where are you going?'

'Here and there. Where else will I go?'

'You need money?'

'No.'

'But take it, take it all, Ib. What am I doing with all that money that Ajju left? I care for your father, that's all I do.'

'Take a holiday. That's the whole point of money. Leave Appoos in the home.'

'So cruel, Ib,' said my mother, 'you were always so cruel.'

I sighed and shook my head.

'Is it so cruel? You're miserable here. You have nobody to talk to. Appoos . . . he's in different worlds.'

'I told you, there's nowhere else he is quiet. Only your room. Shouldn't I be doing everything in my power to make him comfortable and peaceful?'

I wasn't so sure. Is it so noble of man to sacrifice everything for a cause, for another human and in doing so become miserable himself? To waste your entire life because the cruel and laughing bitch Fate threw you into this world with a person whose brain was one way, for no fault of his, or yours?

'I don't know, Amma. But a few days in a home is not going to kill him. And, look at you. A holiday would really do you some good, make you better, and when you come back, you can maybe make this house a little happier. That'll do Ib some good too.'

She closed her eyes and rested her palms on her knees. 'I told you to draw colourful things, didn't I?' she said finally.

'Yes, you did,' I said.

I left soon after. Lunch was tasteless and insufficient. I told mother I would visit once a year, and she smiled as if she knew I was lying to make her feel better.

'Be careful,' she said, 'the city is a dangerous place. The world is a dangerous place.'

'Give Appoos a kiss from me, Ma,' I said, as I went down the steps outside into the hot day of reality.

And as I left I could see her standing on the steps, hands by her sides, looking out into the sun and the dust, and as I turned the corner she waved.

Ib's Endless Search for Satisfaction